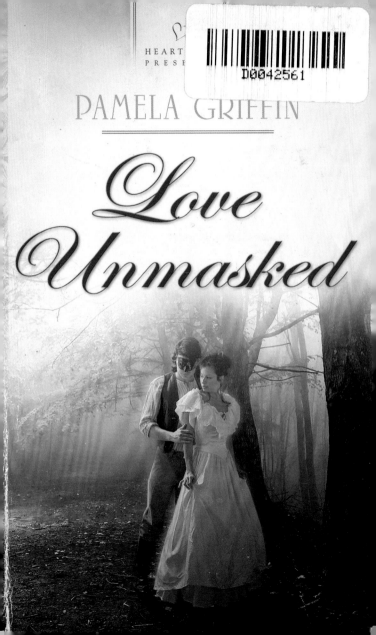

PAMELA GRIFFIN

Love
Unmasked

ISBN-13:978-0-373-48634-2

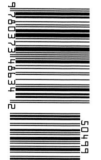

50499

EAN

He stole the chill from her lips, warming them with his breath....

Her eager little moan and the clutch of her hands grabbing his shirt brought him to sudden awareness. Quickly he pulled away, blinking fast to bring his rattled senses together, then dropped his hands from her face.

Pushing himself hurriedly to his feet, he turned his back to her. "That shouldn't have happened." His voice came hoarse.

A brief silence, then the rustle of her skirts grew close.

"It's all right. I—I'm not upset."

Her words came breathless, wondering and awed, and he shook his head, not daring to look at her. His chaotic feelings still teetered on the brink of all they had shared, and he feared that if he took one more glimpse of her sweet face, he would repeat what just happened.

"You have to forget about me. This is wrong. We can't see each other again. For your own safety, you have to forget about me and...stay away." His voice lowered a pitch. "I mean it, Erica. Don't try to find me again."

Before she could protest, he hurried toward his horse and untied it.

"Christopher...?"

He ignored the hurt confusion in her voice, telling himself it was for her own good that he did this, and without a backward glance rode off into the darkness.

PAMELA GRIFFIN

lives in Texas with her family. She fully gave her life to Christ in 1988 after a rebellious young adulthood and owes the fact that she's still alive today to an all-loving and forgiving God and to a mother who steadfastly prayed and had faith that God could bring her wayward daughter "home." Pamela's main goal in writing Christian romance is to help and encourage those who do know the Lord and to plant a seed of hope in those who don't.

Books by Pamela Griffin

HEARTSONG PRESENTS

Love
Unmasked

Pamela Griffin

Heartsong Presents

Dedication and thanks: A huge thanks to my critique partners and helpers! Theo, Peggy, Mom, and my son Joshua. Also to both my sons, Brandon and Joshua, for being such good sports in my hands-on research with a certain captivity scene—thank you! I couldn't have figured it out without you. As always, dedicated to my Lord and Savior, who looks not at outward appearances but only at the heart.

A note from the Author:

I love to hear from my readers! You may correspond with me by writing:

Pamela Griffin
Author Relations
P.O. Box 9048
Buffalo, NY 14240-9048

ISBN-13: 978-0-373-48634-2

LOVE UNMASKED

This edition issued by special arrangement with Barbour Publishing, Inc., 1810 Barbour Drive, Uhrichsville, Ohio, U.S.A.

All scripture quotations are taken from the King James version of the Bible.

Lyrics from: "Crown After Cross" by Frances R. Havergal, pub. 1879

Chapter 1

1890

"Could this day possibly get any worse?"

Erica barely whispered the words as she slipped along the wall and to the edge of the building that housed the dry goods store, hoping she had shaken the deputy who tailed her. She peered around the corner and watched the sandy-haired young man who stood in the middle of the packed dirt street, his eyes darting back and forth in his search. Finally, he turned around the way he'd come, and she let out a relieved breath to see him leave.

With that goal met, Erica pushed onward, in search of a story that would prove her worthy to the *The Chronicle*'s editor and lead him to welcome her into his establishment. She continued down the road and cornered Shamus, the blacksmith. He didn't look happy to see her, but she smiled, trying to put him at ease.

After a tedious, slow beginning, like pouring the thickest remnant of honey from a jar, she was only a few questions into learning about the theft of his tools when Shamus suddenly went silent. Curious, she opened her mouth to ask what the problem was, when she heard another man clear his throat from behind.

"Miss Chandler, there you are. I was wondering where you ran off to."

Groaning inwardly, she thanked Shamus for his time and turned to Ralph. "Really, deputy, you mustn't feel obligated to watch over me. I'm sure there are pursuits far worthier of your skills than to shadow me all over town." She managed a little laugh, though amusement was far from one of her chief emotions at present.

"I made a promise to your father when he put me in charge, that being to keep a watch over you, and I aim to keep my word. Besides, it's a pleasure."

She winced at his clear interest. "Thank you, but I'm perfectly capable of taking care of myself."

"You can never be too careful."

Her answering smile came brittle. "Really, I'm fine." She walked away and heard him follow.

She fumed, barely keeping a pleasant expression on her face toward those she met in passing. She was twenty years of age now, as of last month, not some tot to be coddled. And she doubted that her father, who currently transported a wanted criminal to the state that issued the warrant, intended his request for his deputy to watch over Erica to be taken in the literal sense. That Ralph must play bodyguard, trailing her every move. Not only did his continual presence annoy her, but some people, like Shamus, were less prone to divulge information with a lawman in her wake. Shamus had been in her father's cell more than once for drunken behavior and clearly did not feel comfortable talking around the man who'd often put him there, even if Shamus was the victim this time.

The unproductive afternoon waned into a tenser evening. At last she found reprieve when some boys ran their way, excitedly telling the deputy he was needed where a fight had broken out. Ralph didn't hesitate. Neither did Erica.

As soon as he disappeared down the street with the boys, she hurried in the other direction—to the front of the jailhouse where she had tied her horse, Ginger. Loneliness was often her companion, but Erica needed a hefty dose of peace and solitude after spending an afternoon with Ralph the Watchdog.

The air was cool but not unpleasant, the sun warm—a perfect summer's evening. Once away from town, safe in the countryside, she slowed her horse to a walk and took a deep, relaxing breath of the crisp air laced with evergreens. She lived in what surely could claim to be one of the most beautiful areas of the country and felt delighted that Washington had recently claimed statehood, proud to be one of its citizens.

At the promise of another glorious sunset, she dismounted near a hill that overlooked a long stretch of land flanked on both sides by a forest of tall conifers. In the distance, the sun's dying rays gilded the river that wound throughout the area, lining it in gold, with the peak of a white-capped mountain, glowing pink, rising far beyond it. Walking to the edge of the hill, she gazed at the heavens just beginning to take on a brilliant rose and violet blend.

Perfect.

Her sole suddenly slipped on the ground, the earth breaking apart beneath her boot. She felt a sharp twist of her ankle and lost all balance.

With a shocked cry, she fell to her backside and slid

downhill, her skirts riding up and exposing her bloomers. Small stones bit through her dress. Vainly she grabbed clumps of ground to stop her descent, the grains and grass sifting through her fingers. She landed at the bottom in a bedraggled heap, soiled and breathless. But except for the throb in her ankle and the sting of scraped palms, she seemed unharmed.

Looking up with a groan of dismay, she wiped away the hair sticking to her jaw, at least grateful the hill wasn't so steep that she couldn't crawl her way back upward. She hoped.

"Are you hurt?"

At the unexpected sound of a deep male voice in this wilderness, Erica acted on instinct, grabbing her Derringer from her boot and twisting around to aim.

A stranger stood close to the fringe of trees in the shadows. Tall and lean, broad of shoulder, his appearance suggested strength. He stepped forward into the dying light, and she saw with alarm that he wore a dark mask that covered his forehead and ended below his cheekbones. A gun belt was slung around his hips.

"Don't move or I'll shoot," she warned. "I haven't any money."

"I'm not here to rob you," he assured, lifting his hands in the air, as if in surrender. "I heard you scream when you fell. I only want to make sure you're all right."

"Yes, I'm fine," she clipped. "I don't need your help." The fiery twinge in her ankle told her otherwise. Embarrassed that he saw her fall, and in such an unladylike fashion, she realized her current state and hastily pulled down her skirts, ineffectively brushing the dirt away.

Wishing to keep an eye on his movements, she looked back…

…to see that he had gone.

* * *

Christopher stood at the fringe of forest, using the trees as cover, and watched the feisty brunette, disbelieving her claim that she wasn't hurt. He had heard pain tighten her voice and seen the wince in her brown eyes when she ordered him away. And while he waltzed with danger, even the shadow of death, to let her know of his presence in these dark woods, he couldn't leave an injured woman alone in this wilderness, especially with night fast approaching.

Her ringlets of dark curls were a mass of tangles and dirt almost to her waist, her cheek smeared with soil. After that slide downhill he imagined her dress must be torn. He watched her tuck her small handgun back into her boot and push herself up to stand. She might know how to take care of herself and use a weapon, but in her current state he doubted she could make it uphill. Her condition fragile, she seemed unable to manage the trek. He watched her hobble a few steps and fall.

Not surprised, he shook his head at her stubbornness and left the trees as silently as he first appeared. He had no wish to stare down the barrel of her weapon a second time. Without a word, he came up behind her, turned her around, and slung her over his shoulder like a sack of sugar. She let out a startled gasp and beat on his back with her fists.

"Let me go, you rogue! Put me down—*now!*"

"Stop fighting me. I told you I have no intention of harming you."

His calm warning went unheeded, just as he ignored threat after threat she violently hurled his way.

"Your words don't correspond with your actions." Her replies came more stilted as she struggled for breaths. "You don't call your manhandling harmful? You'll not get away with this, you—you cad. Put me down, *now*, or I'll make sure you regret ever crossing my path." Again she pounded on his lower back.

His arm tightened across her struggling body, until finally he gave an impatient slap to her backside. She froze and gasped in clear shock that he would do such a thing.

"That's better," he said with a satisfied smile. "Use a little sense, miss. You'll only get hurt worse if you cause me to fall. I'm trying to help you."

He headed toward an easier path that led to the top of the slope, one he could manage with the light burden on his shoulder. She had stopped wriggling, but her breathless string of insults and threats continued. Once at the top, he spotted her horse and moved to where she had tethered it to a tree.

"If you don't take your hands off me right now, I'll scream until—"

Her words came to an abrupt halt as he set her down with little finesse atop her saddle.

Clearly astonished, her flushed and damp face a becoming shade of rose, she stared with wide, unblinking eyes of an even richer, deep golden-brown than he'd earlier thought, watching all the while as he untied her horse and pushed the reins into her motionless hands.

"I trust you can find your way home?"

Without awaiting her answer, Christopher turned and trekked back down to the bottom of the hill.

Flustered by the masked stranger's gall, Erica fumed and fretted during the short ride home. By the time she reached the three-story frame house that her father had built on the site of land her mother had dreamed of owning—"away from the bustling town but not so far as to be a daily hindrance in getting there"—Erica's anger had simmered to a low boil. She reasoned that the stranger's aim *had* been noble even if his methods were boorish and crude. On the heels of that assessment, she realized her own conduct had hardly been appropriate for a lady.

Nora, who was more family than cook or housekeeper and had filled the shoes of Erica's mother since her death, dropped her cleaning and rushed to Erica once she hobbled through the door. The matronly woman exclaimed over her soiled clothes, fussed over her overall condition, bandaged her ankle, and cleaned her palms, swabbing some foul home remedy over minor cuts and bruises. Erica wrinkled her nose at the stench but thanked Nora with a hug then reclined on the parlor's divan.

There she spent the next two days.

She talked with the lively Nora, when she could persuade her to take time from chores to rest, immersed herself in twice-read novels to counter boredom, and penned ideas for newsworthy articles. By the time she returned to town, she had no doubt the theft of Shamus's tools would be old news, one of the journalists having snapped up the opportunity.

She wondered if anyone knew of the stranger.

Erica blew a stray curl from her eye as her mind again wandered. No matter how she tried to remain in the present story of choice—whether a novel or her own work—her mind often returned to her strange and awkward meeting with the man in the mask. Now that the passage of time had settled things, calming her emotions, she no longer felt entirely angry with him and was more than a little intrigued.

The sprain turned out to be minor, and on the third morning, Erica could put her full weight on her foot. Confined to the small parlor for two long days that seemed never to end, unable to make the journey up the steep, narrow stairs to her bedroom, she was restless and eager for the wide outdoors. Once she washed and dressed and felt like a member of humankind again, she saddled Ginger and returned to the spot of her fall. Her journalistic spirit assured her a story would be found in this place.

That is, if she could find the stranger.

She frowned when she noticed the small chunk of hill that had crumbled away, resulting in her fall, and dismounted, carefully leading her bay mare down the same path her rescuer had taken to carry her uphill. At the bottom, she tied Ginger to a tree and scouted the area, peering intently at the dense pines from where he once emerged.

"I'm glad to see that you recovered from your fall…"

His deep voice came so unexpectedly she whirled around in shock.

He stood directly behind her, as tall and powerful as before, and she found it hard to take in a breath as she studied him this close. Hair the color of burnished black grew past his ears to his nape, and his eyes glittered a smoky, intense green beyond the mask. The bare hint of a cleft lined a stubborn chin, while a shadow of dark whiskers dusted a determined jaw and the area above the curve of his upper lip. He didn't smile, but his mouth bore a natural tilt at the edge of well-shaped lips, almost mocking. A small hollow of a dimple appeared at the right side. The strangely cut mask, somewhere between charcoal and dark gray, covered his forehead and nose, curving at a gradual slope below his cheekbones and ending near the bottom of his ears. This close, she could tell the mask was made of suede, a thin band of the same material securing it around his head.

"Now, mind telling me why you've come back?" he asked when she continued to stare.

Erica's mind became a sudden blank. Her mouth went dry, and she tried to think. Although she had been looking for him, his sudden and overwhelming presence startled her.

"I…I wish to thank you for the other day. To apologize for my rudeness when you were only trying to help. I realize that now."

His eyes flickered in surprise and suspicion, but he nodded in acknowledgement.

His steady gaze made her strangely flustered, *she*, who rarely grew that way. Her face warmed, and she turned from his intent stare, walking a few short steps from him while searching for appropriate words.

"I wasn't in the best frame of mind; I'd had a bad day. But I shouldn't have said those things, and really, I've *never* spoken like that before. You took me entirely by surprise, though I realize that's no excuse for my bad behavior… ." Erica turned to look at him, her budding smile freezing then fading.

He was nowhere to be seen.

She blinked in utter shock. How did he do that? Once more he had swiftly arrived and departed without her hearing him come or go.

Frustrated that he left in the middle of their conversation and her apology, she took off into the forest, in the direction she assumed he went, the same area he had emerged from two days before.

Here the earth was level bearing plants with tiny flowers, but nothing that could trip her up. The trees grew thicker the farther Erica went, and stretches of mossy ground were bare with the thick boughs blocking sunlight for anything to grow. She left little stacked reminders of nature, pebbles and pinecones for a trail to follow, as she had done as an inquisitive child.

Intrigued by the silent stranger, her determination to find him grew the longer she walked. The mild trickle of a stream met her ears, and she headed in that direction, coming to an area where a shallow brook meandered through the forest. She felt great relief to see him at the water's edge, where he knelt, cupping his hands and taking refreshment. He then pulled a metal flask from his hip and dipped it into the stream.

"Why did you leave?"

For a change, she startled him. His shoulders jerked, and he almost lost hold of the flask. He brought the container back up, screwed the attached stopper on, and replaced it at his hip before answering.

"I thought our conversation was done. You thanked me and offered your apology. I accepted it and left."

He kept his back to her, and she walked to his side. "I wasn't finished talking."

"Oh?" He eyed her warily then stood.

She was tall for a woman but still had to lift her chin to see into his eyes.

"I would have at least offered a farewell if that had been the case, but I had more to say."

His eyes narrowed behind the mask, dropping down the length of her before returning to her face. "You shouldn't be wandering in the forest alone. You could get lost. Could be dangerous, with the wolves and bears about."

He smiled grimly and walked away. She followed.

"I know this land. I grew up nearby. The wolves are only a real threat at night when they hunt, and the bears keep to themselves unless provoked. I know what to do if I ever come across one, and I never go anywhere without my gun. I'm Erica Chandler, by the way."

"What is it you want, Miss Chandler?" he asked impatiently, barely sparing her another glance.

"Well, to begin with, who are you? Why are you here,

all alone, in the forest? And why do you wear a mask if you're not a bandit?"

The questions came fast and furious, spilling from her mouth. His rapid pace never eased, and she found herself running a little to keep up with him.

"You ask a lot of questions."

"You can hardly blame me for being curious, what with our first meeting. I've never seen you around town." She certainly would have remembered him.

"Just passing through."

"And you don't believe in hotels?"

"Don't like them—too noisy with too many intrusive busybodies." He directed a glance in her direction and paused, making it evident he fit her into that class. "Even if I did, I haven't got the money for more than a night or two."

That made sense. "So you have a camp nearby?"

He stopped suddenly, pivoting on his heel, and she did the same. "Why are you so interested?"

"Can you blame me for wanting to know more about the man who helped me out of such an awkward dilemma?" Her face warmed with embarrassment at the memory of how he'd found her. "I owe you a debt of gratitude."

"You don't owe me anything."

His voice came quieter, his manner again calm. She wasn't sure if it was the underlying sadness in his eyes that compelled her to speak or the certain knowledge that he posed no threat, but suddenly the words spilled from her mouth:

"Any time you would like a home-cooked meal, I live just a short piece north of the hill where we met. It's the least I can offer after your gallant rescue." She grinned at the idea of his rescue being gallant, when at the time she'd thought him nothing more than a ruffian.

He somberly stared at her a moment longer before he nodded once then walked away.

Feeling slighted yet again, this time Erica did not follow.

Christopher returned to his campsite, mulling over his terse conversation with the lively Erica Chandler. He hardly had been polite but hadn't asked for her company either. After spending more than a year in forced solitude, the long minutes in her presence had been uncomfortable though not unpleasant. He missed being among people, aware he would never again enjoy that benefit. Once he'd been even-tempered, able to converse with anyone.

All that had changed after the fire.

He couldn't risk attempting to socialize with any of Barretts Grove's citizens, though Christopher doubted the young Miss Chandler posed a true threat. And her offer of a home-cooked meal did sound tempting after endless months of nothing but canned salmon, beans, berries, and whatever small game he could catch and roast over a campfire.

The last occasion he associated with anyone had been necessarily brief, at a general store in Seattle. And he had ridden in and out of the city before anyone knew of his presence there. Like Miss Chandler, the elderly woman behind the counter had fretted and feared he meant to rob her when she saw his mask. She had shown surprise when he slapped two dollars on the counter for the items needed to replenish his stores then tugged down the brim of his hat and left. He had always been a fast runner, faster than anyone in his hometown, and the need to hone such swiftness and learn to move with silence became imperative for a life on the lam.

The mask not only kept him from being recognized, especially by any lawmen, but also prevented others from witnessing the grotesque scars left behind. He would never again reveal the knowledge of their existence or the sight of them to anyone. He had seen horror and revulsion in the eyes of those few close to him that he once so foolishly trusted.

Never again would he make that same mistake.

His mood somber and dark, he cooked a can of beans over the fire and stared into the low flames, the memory of that other fire that raged in the winter of last year never far from his thoughts.

That fire had robbed him of his life, destroying everything he cared about. Stealing from him his hope for a happy future, the trust of his loved ones, even his good name—and leaving behind its cruel mark to brand him in a way he would carry for the remainder of his days. He would never be the same, could never again go out among society and belong, even without the constant threat of his identity being uncovered and the subsequent fear of having a noose tied around his neck.

Justice wasn't good enough, not that anyone but him was seeking it. And he had tracked his enemy from Oregon to this remote area of Washington State.

Only revenge would satisfy his keen desire to make the true scoundrel who had framed him for murder, theft, and arson pay...

And he would pay dearly. Christopher would see to that.

Chapter 2

Erica's fingers gently struck the keys of the piano in an even flow, her voice joining in with the sweet melody.

Whenever she felt upset, she turned to this method of comfort, singing hymns she learned as a child. Often she was asked to sing a solo at social gatherings and church meetings, her skill praised by many, and she always complied, happily sharing with others the talent God gave her.

She still smarted from the stranger's curt manner two days ago and felt disappointed by his unsatisfactory replies to her questions. But as her voice flowed to join the notes, singing of God's mighty power, the message soothed her soul.

On the third stanza, a strange prickle of awareness made her pause, sensing she wasn't alone. Her hands stilled, and she looked to the parlor door. No one had entered, but the feeling didn't go away. She turned on the bench, her attention shifting to the partially open window.

The masked stranger stood there, half hidden by bushes. He looked at her in awe, his mouth parted in surprise, the overall image of him somehow vulnerable.

Why that last thought should surface, Erica wasn't sure. He didn't look any less powerful or in command than before…

Or any less likely to disappear.

She didn't hesitate and hurried outdoors.

He turned to her as, with an uncertain smile, she moved toward him.

"Hello," she said brightly, somewhat nervous.

For the first time since she'd known him, he also smiled, though it didn't come across entirely genuine. The depths of sadness had not left his beautiful, silvery-green eyes that had haunted her slumber, and her heart clenched, wondering what tragedy he must have suffered. He appeared to be in his midtwenties but bore an ancient look in his eyes, as if he'd seen untold horrors.

"Good afternoon, Miss Chandler," he said and tipped his hat with all the mannerly conduct she thought he lacked. "I'd like to take you up on your offer of a meal, if it's still available?"

"Of course." She just resisted grabbing his arm and leading him inside. "But why didn't you come to the door?" She walked toward it, relieved when he fell into step beside her.

"I heard you playing and didn't think you'd hear a knock. You sing like an angel."

Erica smiled, her skin warming with a rosy flush. As many times as she'd heard that, the compliment never affected her so greatly or meant so much as it did now.

"Nora, the woman who cooks for us, is in town. But she taught me my way around the kitchen."

He hesitated. "You're sure it won't be any trouble?"

"Of course not." She wasn't about to let him out of sight. "Come on back with me."

Once in the kitchen, at her invitation, he sat at the small table while she sliced bread baked that morning and set out a slab of butter. A glance at the wood-burning stove showed that Nora had prepared a stew. One taste from a spoon assured Erica it was ready.

As she sliced and stirred and ladled, also putting on a pot of coffee, she kept the conversation alive with little anecdotes of her life, her past, and their home. He offered a question now and then, always related to what she just said. With their last two encounters in mind, she was astonished by the ease of their conversation.

"Papa bought me the piano the Christmas after Mama died of a fever. I was twelve. He ordered it the month before she passed. I couldn't believe it when I saw it. It was and still is the most wonderful gift I have ever received." Her voice went soft with wonder. "He's always supported my musical abilities even though he's tone deaf. Mother couldn't carry a tune either. It's a wonder I can even sing," she added with a laugh.

He smiled, accepting the bowl she set before him with quiet thanks.

"Have you ever thought of singing as a professional career?"

"A career? *Singing?*" She shook her head at such a thought. "The only call for singers in these parts is in places of ill repute, and I have no wish to be a saloon girl. Besides, I prefer to sing only when I wish to and not have it daily expected of me. It's a joy to me, a comfort." She thought about telling him of her true career pursuit, wondering what he would think of a woman journalist. Perhaps he might help her out and be amenable to the idea of giving her a story.

She suddenly tilted her head in shock. "You know, I just realized—"

A knock at the front door interrupted, preventing her from asking his name.

She blew out a breath of frustration. "I wonder who that could be. Please, do enjoy your meal. I'll be back shortly."

At the kitchen door, she gave one last parting glance over her shoulder to assure herself he had not disappeared and was really still sitting at her table then hurried to open the front door.

"Deputy, hello." She managed to hide her dismay. "What brings you all the way to this side of the woods?"

He tipped his hat with an uncertain smile. "I received a wire from your pa. Thought you should know that he's been detained. He's not sure when he'll be back."

"Oh. Well, thank you for coming to deliver the message."

"Of course. I told your pa I'd take care of you." He looked beyond her shoulder, his pale blue eyes intent. "Everything all right? Something sure smells good."

She sighed. "Everything is fine. Nora made a mutton stew for dinner."

"She should take over at Grace's restaurant. The fare isn't half as good there."

At his obvious hint, she felt she had no choice. "Won't you come in and join us?"

She wondered what he would say about her masked stranger's presence in her kitchen.

"Thank you." He stepped in and took off his hat, smoothing his hair. "Don't mind if I do."

She took his hat and hung it on the rack then led Ralph back to the kitchen. Opening her mouth to make what weak introduction she could, when she didn't even know

her other guest's name, she stopped inside the door in surprised disappointment.

Her masked stranger had gone.

Ralph stepped around her and took his chair. "Everything all right?" he asked yet again, making her want to
scream.

"Yes, of course." She moved to the back door, opening it. There was no sign of the man from the forest anywhere, not that she should have expected any differently,
what with his skill of vanishing so quickly.

"You said 'us.'"

At the curious bent to his words, she glanced at Ralph.
"Pardon?"

"When you invited me inside. You said 'us.'"

"Oh. Well, Nora left for a short spell." She glanced back
out the door in the other direction, uncertain as to why, but
feeling she shouldn't mention her earlier guest.

"This sure is good." Ralph again spoke from behind
her, and she turned, watching him eat the meal intended
for her stranger. He slathered butter on a slice of cornbread
and took a bite.

"The coffee should be ready soon," she said dismally.

He nodded and looked at her. "Aren't you going to have
some? I'm sorry, but I was so hungry I couldn't stop from
eating what you already dished out."

Her smile came genuine at his shamed confession.
"That's all right, deputy. No need to apologize."

"Please, won't you call me Ralph?"

His soft-spoken question made his interest plain, and
Erica grew uneasy.

She had known the man six months, since he'd come to
town. And though he was handsome and kind, his overbearing nature and constant demand to have things done
his way where it concerned Erica only made her want to

run in the other direction. She couldn't think of one occasion when she'd felt completely at ease in Ralph's presence. But he had helped her out a few times in the spirit of friendship, and her father must think highly of him to have made him his deputy. She thought of Ralph more as her father's aid rather than a good friend. At the same time, she didn't wish to hurt his feelings.

"If you'd like," she agreed but didn't offer the same liberty.

Whether or not he noticed her omission, she didn't speculate.

She pulled down a second bowl from the cupboard, more to give herself something to do than for any true desire to eat. The atmosphere had grown uncomfortable, an opposition to the peace she'd earlier felt before Ralph made his appearance. And her mind wandered outdoors, back to the forest with the stranger…who oddly, at some point, she had come to think of as hers.

Christopher rushed to where his horse was tethered and hidden from view of the house. Untying the rope, he took up the reins and mounted, guiding the animal back into the woods. His stomach growled in protest, and he resigned himself to the prospect of another evening of cold canned salmon, though both his tins and his funds were running low.

In Oregon, not long after he began a life on the run, he came across a nearly blind, elderly widow. His act of chopping firewood and doing other chores around her cabin for a week had resulted in her paying him a tidy sum from her stash that her miner husband left her. She told Christopher she sensed that he needed it more and she had little use for money since she felt she soon would be meeting her Maker. He had not refused her generous offer, and she had even given him her husband's horse. After that incident, when his funds bled dry or the weather grew too cold, he would approach the owner of a homestead far from a town, immediately explaining the mask as protecting a bad condition of his face, so as not to get shot, adding that it wasn't contagious. Usually he would find shelter in a barn and enough work to fill the small drawstring purse he carried around his neck, tucked inside his shirt, enough to take him through a few months. Only once had he nearly been caught, near the boundary of Washington, when the visiting sheriff of that community came to pay his respects to a friend. Christopher had ridden away in the nick of time.

He had hoped to find similar work at Miss Chandler's, but that was now out of the question, and he felt grateful he'd had the foresight to furtively slip outside the kitchen door at the sound of the boisterous male voice.

He had seen a partial view of her guest before he'd had a chance to spot Christopher. The silver star on his vest had gleamed in the sun, and by his conversation with the young Miss Chandler, the deputy knew her well.

Still shaken by his narrow escape and the identity of her guest, Christopher scowled at how close he'd come to being caught. That she knew the lawman concerned him, and he worried that she might reveal Christopher's presence without knowledge of the hornets' nest she would rouse. He was so close now. The previous night he had followed his enemy while keeping himself hidden in shadows.

The prey he hunted favored towns and crowds, the noisier the better, and rarely kept to himself. Last night Christopher had watched a lady of the evening accompany his foe upstairs to his room, ending Christopher's chance for the imminent confrontation.

To devise a way to get the wretch alone, away from town, presented a problem. But he was more than up to the challenge. His sole aim in a life destroyed was to have that man in his clutches, to then witness his shock and terror, such as Christopher had known, before he exacted revenge—

And as surely as he lived and breathed, his day would come.

Chapter 3

Erica rode into town with the hope that someone else might have seen, or at least know of, her masked stranger. It had been three days since he vanished from her home, and though she had revisited the site where they met each of those days, he never again appeared.

She had no wish to betray his whereabouts; for a reason she couldn't understand, she felt a need to protect such information. Whenever they met, she sensed in his quiet, sometimes curt manner a deep, hidden sorrow, certain a tragedy must have led him to live as a recluse in those woods, and she wanted to help, though she had no idea how to go about doing so. She no longer thought him a criminal. The mask and why he should wear it remained a mystery, but if he wanted to harm or rob her, he had been given ample opportunities. That he'd done neither and instead put her welfare first, seeing to her safety, proved his motives weren't evil. She assumed he left quietly after the deputy's arrival because he thought he might be in the way, as disturbingly familiar as Ralph had acted and as loud as his voice sometimes carried.

But the persistent need to know more, a sometimes wretched trait she'd been born with, compelled Erica to seek out what she could find. She didn't even know his name!

Newcomers arrived to these parts often, either just passing through or loggers and miners seeking work. Only one man she knew wore a mask and for that purpose could be described as unique—which is how she would frame her question, in the hope it would spark a memory about a man in a mask.

The elderly men around the pickle barrel at Hardy's General Store had seen no one to fit the description. Nor was her curiosity of any unique newcomers in town quenched by the two women she knew and greeted who were partaking of lunch at the small restaurant. At Ruby's boardinghouse, the wise old woman who ran the place paused in sweeping her stoop to nod.

"Unique? Hmph. Well, I don't know if I'd call him that. A man came here more 'n' a week ago, wanted a room. Nasty sort. Dressed like a dandy and smelled of whiskey. Wasn't at all timid to show his bankroll, but don't want that sort in my establishment or near my granddaughter." She shook her index finger at Erica. "Nothing but trouble, that one."

He hardly sounded like the same man, and she noted Ruby made no mention of a mask—something that surely would come up when describing a unique newcomer. But she would leave no stone unturned. "Do you know where he is now?"

"A sweet thing like you should stay away from the likes

of him, Miss Erica. Your pa wouldn't be happy to learn you were consorting with that sort."

"From the way you describe him, I doubt he's the man I'm looking for, but I'd like to know all the same."

Ruby sniffed in derision. "I told him he'd have better luck at the hotel. They cater to his kind. Though it wouldn't surprise me if he spent his days gambling in the devil's new drinking hole. Saw him heading there after he left my place. I guarantee that wad of bills he flashed came from a life of perdition."

Erica glanced farther up the street toward the recently built saloon.

"Then there was that other man…." Ruby said in a tone of recalling something forgotten. "Liam Aldridge, I believe was his name. But I wouldn't call him unique. Seemed well off. Quiet sort. Stayed here only a week before he took up in the hotel." She sniffed. "Vile place, don't know why he wanted to go there."

Erica thanked Ruby for her time. The woman nodded, the look she gave Erica concerned, but she said nothing else and went back to her sweeping.

Outside the drinking establishment, Erica hesitated. As a moral young woman, she would never step foot inside. As a hopeful prospective journalist, she might have to resort to such measures.

If they could read her thoughts at this moment, Nora would be mortified, her father livid.

Erica hesitated with the idea, noting two men who often spent time in her father's cell for disorderly behavior loitering on the stoop and now ogling her with narrow-eyed curiosity. These men and others knew not to stir up trouble when it came to Erica, due to her father being the sheriff. She had just made up her mind to march up the steps and question them when two men walked toward her from the street.

"My, my, they grow them pretty here in Washington." The more handsome of the two took off his hat with a cavalier bow. "Jake Millstone, at your service. You look as if you're lost, miss. Perhaps I can be of assistance?"

She looked at the man and frowned. Despite his boyish good looks and attempt at charm, a hint of something dark flashed in his twinkling eyes that made her uneasy, and she didn't return his introduction.

"I highly doubt it," she replied, "since I know the layout of Barretts Grove like the back of my hand."

This won a slight chuckle from Mr. Millstone's companion. Tall and gaunt, with brown hair and a drooping mustache, he also appeared as if he was in his twenties. She didn't recognize either of them and wondered if these were the men Ruby spoke of.

He awkwardly tipped his hat to her. "Good day, miss. I must go. Jake." He nodded to his friend and left.

Erica curiously watched him go, noting he seemed in a hurry, and wondered if his swift departure was due to her presence.

"Would you care for an escort?" Mr. Millstone captured her attention again. "A young woman like you shouldn't walk alone, and I have time to spare."

Like her? What did *that* mean? Was it a slight?

Annoyed by his familiar attitude, Erica stepped away. "I have no need of an escort, sir. My father is the sheriff. I learned to shoot when I was twelve and can knock a tin can off a post at twenty paces. I assure you I won't come to any harm. Now, if you'll excuse me I have business to attend to."

"Of course." He seemed surprised by her accounting

of her abilities and tipped his hat, his manner a bit cold at her rebuff, then turned and walked back into the saloon.

Shaking her head in wry disbelief at the encounter that left her feeling like the quarry that got away, she decided to forego questioning the two men on the stoop and instead put as much distance between her and Mr. Millstone as possible. She wasn't sure he was the same man Ruby had referred to—he certainly dressed well but hadn't smelled of spirits. And the other man had practically run off at her presence and didn't seem to fit the description of a wastrel either. Though she had learned never to judge on appearances alone.

Yet neither man was the reason she was here and therefore held no interest to her.

As she often did, she found herself inside the small building of *The Chronicle*. The racket coming from the printing press vied with the exchange of men's voices as they readied the next edition for publication. The heady, sweet smell of black ink on fresh paper countered the rank odor of old cigar smoke. Upon seeing her, Mr. Mahoney, the editor, grabbed a cigar from the box on his desk and lit it, clearly hoping to force her exit. But she was not deterred.

Vaguely she heard the words "A stranger mask I've never seen" from a man in deep discussion with his co-worker, neither of them having yet noticed her. She eagerly advanced.

"You've seen the man in the mask, too?" she asked, lifting her voice to be heard and momentarily forgetting her decision not to reveal her stranger.

Mr. Nilsson sat back and laid down his pen, a grin quirking his thin lips.

"Miss Chandler, what a surprise," he said dryly. "A man in a mask? No, can't say I've seen such a fellow."

"But I heard you! You were talking about a man wearing a mask."

His gray brows lifted. "I was telling Lou, here, about a masquerade ball my wife forced me to attend while we were visiting her sister in California, as the mayor's wife has now announced she plans to hold one. The mask I spoke of belonged to a female. Not sure what you're referring to—a man in a mask?"

"Yes, in the forest. He comes and goes so silently and swiftly, I never hear him." She spoke her thoughts then realized how bizarre they sounded when aired aloud.

As expected, the men laughed. The press went quiet. The two burly youths manning it stopped in their task to gawk at her as if she'd lost all sense.

"I think that wild imagination of yours is the real culprit, Miss Chandler."

"Culprit? Oh, but I never said he was a troublemaker."

"Maybe he's the ghost of a bandit miner, and that's why he vanishes so quickly," Lou suggested with a wide smile full of browning teeth. Another round of guffaws filled the room at his remark.

Her face burned with embarrassed indignation. "He's no ghost. He's real. He came to my aid, practically saved my life."

"Sure he did. Maybe in your dreams."

"Or more likely in your book of fairy tales."

"Miss Chandler." The editor spoke above his workers. "Stories of pretense won't land you a job here either. As I've told you, time and again, I *don't hire women reporters*." He took a long puff of his cigar, blowing the smoke in her direction. "Now I suggest you go home and take up some worthy occupation to fill your hours, like knitting. I have a paper to run. Boys, carry on."

Erica stiffened her shoulders and regarded her tormentors. "Gentlemen," she said, frost coating her polite but stiff farewell. She turned in a dignified manner, leaving the building in high dudgeon.

She didn't know if she felt more upset that no one would believe her about her masked stranger or irritated by yet another refusal to be taken seriously.

To her chagrin, her day took a further downslide as she caught sight of Jake Millstone across the street. He noticed her, hesitated, and approached.

"What a coincidence meeting you again so soon," he greeted with a nervous smile.

Odd, she would have thought him to be the sort who always exuded overconfidence.

"We got off to a bad start. I apologize if I said anything to offend. It wasn't my intent."

He seemed sincere, and she faintly nodded. "I accept."

"Yet you still look upset."

She had no desire to review what just happened, especially with a stranger, and managed a courteous smile. "It's nothing to do with you."

"It might help to talk." He paused. "If I may be so bold, might I ask your name?"

"Erica Chandler. I'm sorry, Mr. Millstone." She shook her head. "I'm really not fit company at the moment and should be getting home."

"Then might I offer you a ride? My wagon's at the livery. It won't take but a moment to hitch it up."

"No, that's quite all right. I have my horse. Good day, Mr. Millstone."

She began walking toward the jailhouse.

He fell into step beside her, and she looked at him in surprise.

"Since you said you know the town well, I thought you might enlighten me about the people who live in it?"

His expression was sheepish. "I've only been here a short time."

"Oh. I suppose I could do that." She still didn't feel entirely comfortable with him after their first encounter, but she was a firm advocate of second chances.

Once they arrived at the jailhouse, Ralph walked outside. He narrowed his eyes at her self-appointed escort.

"Everything all right here, Erica?"

A little startled to hear him speak so informally, she took a moment to answer.

"Yes, *deputy*," she stressed the word. "Everything is fine."

His face flushed as he received her opposing message to his taking the liberty. Her escort stepped forward, putting out his hand. "Jake Millstone."

Ralph somberly shook the man's hand, eyeing his pin-striped suit. "Deputy Michaels. You're not from around these parts, are you?"

"No, sir. I'm an investor with the Great Northern Railway."

"If you'll be excusing me, gentlemen, I'd best be heading home." Erica moved toward Ginger and untied her from the post.

It was clear from the look Ralph gave that he wished her to stay, but both men bid her farewell.

She rode out of town, wishing only to find solace so that she could lick her wounds. Tomorrow, she would likely be ready to tackle the world of journalism again, but at the moment she struggled with doubt that she could ever prove herself worthy enough to gain a position at Mr. Mahoney's paper. That is, if she could override the editor's prejudice of women journalists.

Before she quite realized it, she came to the hill. She found herself dismounting and tied Ginger to a tree then walked to the bottom. Clasping her wrist behind her, she wandered the grassy expanse, staring at the glimpse of river that glimmered silver in the distance and the slope of the snow-covered mount beyond it.

"You seem to make a habit of coming here," a deep, masculine voice said from behind. "Is there a reason?"

At his smooth timbre she gave a little shiver, the feeling not at all unpleasant. No longer surprised by his quiet entrance, having hoped for just such an encounter, she smiled to herself and turned to greet her stranger.

"Yes, there is. But first, I would like to know your name."

Chapter 4

Christopher didn't know what to make of the fearless Erica Chandler or of her persistence to show up near his camp. He struggled against his attraction to the woman, though he wasn't surprised by it—what man in his right mind wouldn't consider her a beauty? She had that indescribable something, perhaps due to her lively, excitable nature, that made her skin and eyes and even her wild clusters of curls radiate with light. When in her company, he felt alive for the first time in over a year. At the same time, hearing her sing had oddly calmed his soul. But none of that mattered.

He remained leery of being near her, after learning the identity of her friend, the deputy. Yet after what felt like a lifetime of forced solitude, he'd found pleasure in her company after she made him feel welcome in her home. The past few days, he had curiously watched her from the cover of the trees once she arrived at the bottom of the hill.

She always came in the evening and stayed through sunset, sitting in the grass amid the violet wildflowers. The first time, he'd heard her horse whinny and had gone to investigate. The last three occasions, including this evening, he'd made it a point to be in the vicinity near the close of day, curious if she would return. It had been difficult not to go to her, but he had resisted. He couldn't name the strong urge that brought him out of hiding this time; it felt like more than just attraction or desire. The need to talk with her again, to be close to her, had been fierce, and against all good judgment he had relented and come forward.

She lifted her brows. "You do have a name?"

"It's Christopher."

When he said nothing else, she gave a curious smile. "Nothing more?"

"No."

The need to conceal his identity prevented him from tacking on a surname.

She took a few pensive steps, looking toward the beginning of a sunset. Quickly she looked back as if afraid he might disappear.

"Why did you leave so suddenly the other day? You left without saying good-bye."

Did he imagine the hurt in her voice?

"You had company. I didn't want to get in the way."

She regarded him oddly. "*You* were my company. I didn't invite the deputy to call."

Her explanation offered only momentary relief when he remembered why he couldn't allow matters to advance in whatever this was that *should not* be budding between them. *Dangerous*, was the word that came to mind. Dangerous and addictive. And by her presence here these past few days, he hadn't been the only one unable to stay away.

"I should go." The only wise decision he'd made all day, he moved to retrace his steps to the solitude of the forest.

"Wait." She stopped him before he could fully turn from her. "You asked if I had a reason for coming. I haven't yet told you what it is."

Christopher nodded impatiently. Her thick, brown ringlets had begun to take on a rosy golden cast from the skies, her face glowing with the same hue, and her dark eyes sparkled. He swallowed hard.

"Since you never got your dinner," she said with quiet charm, "I'd like to invite you again."

He opened his mouth to decline, but she hurried on as if expecting him to.

"It's only fair. I promised you a home-cooked meal you have yet to enjoy."

"I'm not sure that's such a good idea anymore…"

Her brows drew together. "Why not? You were willing to come to my house before."

"I don't want to get in the way again."

"You weren't in the way last time. I sincerely doubt the deputy will make another house call, if that's what's worrying you. He rarely comes by." She drew close, to where she initially stood when he'd come up behind her. "The truth is, with my father out of town, it's been lonely, and I would love the company. Please say you'll reconsider."

He was a fool for letting things get this far, but he didn't like to see distress replace the shine in her eyes. "I'll think about it."

A hopeful smile edged her lips, and for seconds more than he ought to, he focused on their rosy fullness.

"Tomorrow then? At this time? I would ask you to come now, but I first need to speak with Nora, so she'll be sure to have enough prepared."

He gave a noncommittal nod.

"All right." She hesitated. "I could play a few tunes for you afterward, if you'd like."

She seemed loath to go, but with dusk closing in she would need to leave soon. He smiled in parting. "Good night, Miss Chandler. Be careful getting home."

"I'm always careful… Good night…Christopher."

He heard her quiet farewell once he turned to go, followed by the quieter add-on of his name that she said after he began walking back to the forest edge. She sounded both shy and determined, an odd combination. Odder still was the jolt it gave Christopher's heart to hear her whisper his name.

"Looking out the window every few minutes won't make him appear any faster."

If he appears at all, Erica thought in dismay.

She withheld an impatient sigh and smiled. "Dinner smells delicious. You outdid yourself, Nora."

She laughed. "You helped."

"But you did most of it. I just hope my company arrives before the meat dries out."

Erica picked up a book, sat on the divan, and waited, forcing herself not to run to the window for yet another look. The minute hand moved another few inches along the face of the mantel clock. The parlor grew darker as the sun dipped behind the spires of the towering evergreens.

"Did he say what time he would be here?"

"Actually…" Erica closed the book on a dreary chapter and shook her head with her reluctant admission. "He never said for certain he was coming at all." She set the book down on her lap. "I suppose it's just us again, Nora."

"I wouldn't be so sure of that."

Erica quickly looked up in confusion, noting Nora now

stared out the window, a smile on her face. "I think that might be your young gentleman friend now."

Her familiar words as much as her announcement brought Erica's heartbeats to a rapid clip. She stood abruptly, the book dropping to the floor, then frowned at her clumsiness and stooped to pick it up.

"That mask is a strange one," Nora pondered. "It must cover more than half his face. And you say he never told you why he wears it? Could it be he had an accident?"

"I don't know." Erica replaced the book on the table, having also come to such a conclusion. It would help explain the trace of sorrow in his eyes. Yet she had made up her mind not to ask until he was ready to tell her. She didn't wish to give him any reason to withdraw and secret himself away again. From what little she knew of her masked man, whom she no longer called a stranger, she knew that asking such a question could do it.

Because she had not wanted Nora to stare upon meeting Christopher and make him ill at ease, Erica had told her about the mask in advance. At Nora's instant alarm, which had increased when she learned he made his home alone in the forest, Erica had also felt the need to relate Christopher's role in helping her up the hill, having left him out of her story completely the first time she told Nora of her fall. That had soothed Nora, somewhat, who said she doubted that anyone who would aid an injured woman and demand nothing in return could be a real threat.

Erica nervously patted the ringlets she had piled on top of her head, having allowed only a small number of them to cascade down to her nape. A few of the most unruly ones had already escaped their pins. She wrinkled her nose with a grimace and yanked and wrapped and adjusted her rowdy hair—when the knock came at the door. Her heart pounded, and she froze. The moment she'd been waiting more than a day for, and her limbs suddenly refused to move.

Nora glanced her way. "You collect yourself; I'll let him in."

Erica took in a deep breath then followed. She arrived in the receiving area as Nora motioned Christopher inside.

Greetings and introductions made, Erica noticed how hard Nora tried not to glance at his mask, which ironically made the situation as uncomfortable as if Nora had come right out and asked. The three stood and looked among one another, while Erica desperately tried to make her mind work to form a greeting and ease the gathering tension.

She smiled at him. "I wasn't sure you would come."

"I almost didn't."

"Oh? Well, I'm glad you changed your mind. Please, come inside." She led him to the adjoining room, Nora in their wake. "Won't you take a seat?"

He moved to the end of the settee. Both women nervously smiled. Erica took a seat beside him.

"It's a lovely evening," she began. "For a while I thought it might rain."

All three struggled to avoid the elephant in the parlor in the shape of a dark mask. After more awkward conversation with regard to stormy weather and their gratitude that the dry season had at last arrived, another taut silence arose.

"I imagine you must be wondering about this," Christopher said at last, giving a careless wave to his face, his voice sounding tight. Erica couldn't help but nod, noting Nora did the same.

"My skin, that is my face, is highly sensitive to sunlight. A malady I've learned to cope with."

"I'm sorry," Erica sympathized, neither she nor Nora bringing up the fact that what little of the sun there had

been approached its final descent, with a huge dense forest providing a wall to the west, and he was indoors now.

"That is unfortunate. I suppose we all have our crosses
to bear." Nora acted somewhat flustered, though Erica
sensed she tried to be reassuring. "Come to the dining
room, both of you. The table is laid and ready."

They moved to the room across from the parlor. Nora
whisked toward the kitchen to bring the food.

"Do you need help?" Erica called after her, a little
breathless at the thought of sharing a room alone with
Christopher, even briefly. Strange, considering that in the
forest alone with him, even that day he'd sat in her kitchen,
she'd been quite bold and not so shy.

"I can manage." Nora's response came as she disappeared through the door.

Erica moved to her seat. To her shock, Christopher also
moved, his hands taking the corners of her chair and pulling it out for her. She blinked in astonishment, noting a
wry trace of amusement in his eyes.

"I'm not a complete cad, Miss Chandler. My mother
did raise me with a few good manners, little chance I've
had to put them to use."

Her face warmed with the memory of the many insult-
ing names she had called him the first day they'd met.
Rogue, cad, scoundrel...

"To be fair, you did sneak up on me once I thought you
were gone, and without telling me why," she said as she
took a seat.

He moved around the table to sit across from her, where
another plate had been laid. "I would have thought that
would have been obvious, with the way you were limping
and trying to get up that hill."

"Yes, well, you can hardly blame me for jumping to the
wrong conclusion after you threw me over your shoulder

like some ill-mannered barbarian who'd been bred among wolves."

The words came light, without rancor. A grin teased his lips and hers as well.

"So now I'm a Neanderthal, and the beasts are my kin?"

"For all I know that might be the case, since you've chosen to make your home in the forest, and I have nothing else to go on."

The light in his eyes dimmed, and she frowned. It had not been her intent to hurt or belittle him.

"Tell me about your mother," she inquired kindly, feeling that topic must be safe since he'd brought her up.

"She died when I was a boy. My pa died, too."

"I'm sorry," Erica commiserated.

"It was a bad winter that year. My grandfather raised me."

"Does he live nearby?"

Christopher shook his head. "He died in the spring of last year."

"Have you no other family?" Her voice came softer.

"No, it's just me."

Her heart twisted at his circumstances, feeling his pain as if it were her own. It was on the tip of her tongue to assure him that she would always be there for him, and she just refrained from speaking it, wondering in surprise where such a startling thought had come from.

Nora appeared with a platter of roast duck and red currant jelly and, in her other hand, a bowl of cooked green vegetables. She took the chair beside Erica, and they bowed their heads to say grace. Erica noted Christopher's slight hesitation before he followed suit, the silent movement of his lips an assurance that he wasn't a heathen and had taken part in the traditional dinner prayer before.

They passed the meal in quiet conversation involving

the news about town, and the former ease she felt in the kitchen with him days ago returned. After dessert, Nora suggested that Erica entertain Christopher in the parlor while she tended to the dishes. Her words assured Erica that she approved of Christopher; otherwise she never would leave their sight.

"I promised I would play for you," Erica said, somewhat bashful at the idea. She had only played for her father and Nora before this, except on the occasion when Erica hadn't realized she'd had an audience in Christopher. Mrs. Bristol, a former piano teacher, accompanied Erica when she sang in public.

His smoky green eyes glowed soft in hesitant request. "Will you sing for me?"

"Of course." Her words again came uncertain, as if she'd never had an audience to hear her voice, and she realized how earnestly she hoped for his approval. "What would you like me to sing?"

"I'll leave that up to you."

"All right then. Please, take a seat."

She sat at the piano as he sank into the divan.

Tilting her head, she thought a moment then played and sang:

> *"Light after darkness, gain after loss,*
> *Strength after weakness, crown after cross;*
> *Sweet after bitter, hope after fears,*
> *Home after wandering, praise after tears..."*

With her eyes closed, Erica continued with the rest of the melody, so caught up in the beautiful words of reassurance she didn't realize Christopher had come to stand beside her until suddenly she felt his warmth near her back.

Startled, she ceased playing and twisted around to look at him.

He stared at her in wonder, his eyes moist as he stepped to her side and took her small hand in his large one. Stunned by his response and the physical contact, she did not resist as he drew her up to stand.

"How did you know?" he asked hoarsely.

"Know what?" She could barely think.

"That 'Crown After Cross' was my mother's favorite hymn?"

"I didn't." She found no words to admit it was her favorite, too.

"I think you must be an angel," he whispered.

She felt unable to move, even to *breathe*, while time itself seemed to stop its advance.

He studied her eyes, finding something there that made him flinch in amazement, his manner then becoming intent. His index finger curled beneath her chin and tipped it slightly, his touch so light as hardly to be noticed.

Gentle as a whisper, his lips brushed hers, hesitant, as if waiting for her to pull away, and she realized some hidden part of her had anticipated this. His skin was warm, the caress of his mouth like the brush of a feather and sweet with the lingering taste of cider. The leather of his mask softly grazed her cheek as he leaned in deeper. She breathed a little involuntary whimper of need, squeezing his hand and wishing he would draw her into his strong arms.

He released her swiftly and pulled away, his expression stunned and troubled.

"That was all wrong," he said, his voice husky.

"Wrong?" She could hardly speak for her dismay, thinking it had felt so *right*.

"I shouldn't have taken that liberty. Forgive me."

At his somber apology, the dazed warmth from their

shared intimacy dissolved, and she came to her senses with a snap, the situation now clear and awkward. No doubt, Nora would not approve of her kissing a man she'd barely known for almost two weeks or consider it appropriate parlor entertainment. Strange that Erica felt as if she'd known Christopher all her life.

"Please, don't apologize," she managed, her voice hardly sounding like her own. "I didn't exactly push you away."

Curiously he regarded her. "Why didn't you?"

"Do you wish I had?"

"For your sake, yes."

She shook her head in confusion. "I don't understand."

"You don't want to get involved with the likes of me, Erica."

The gentle sound of her name on his lips warmed her to her toes, and she realized that when coming from him, she welcomed the informality.

"Maybe I do."

What might have happened next, they never found out. For at that moment, the sound of a horse and rider broke through the heady, thickened atmosphere, and Christopher swiftly turned his eyes to the window.

"Who would that be at this time of night? Are you expecting someone else?"

"No." Erica moved to the pane of glass. "It's my father!" she exclaimed, turning back to Christopher, her smile wide and relieved. "He's returned from transferring a prisoner to Oregon. His trip was delayed—which is why the deputy came the other day, to tell me that."

Christopher warily stared at her. "Transferring a prisoner?"

"He's the sheriff, and a better one you'll never find. I know you'll like him once you two meet—"

"No!"

The shock from her announcement riddled through Christopher's soul with the precision of a round of bullets, shattering what little peace had remained after the spontaneous kiss. At his vigorous reply, she studied him in clear surprise, and he forced a calm he was far from feeling.

"It wouldn't be wise for you to present him with a strange man in your company on his first night home."

Her face cleared, and she smiled. "I don't think he would mind that I invited you to dinner. I'm not a child in constant need of a chaperone. Besides, Nora is in the next room."

"After what just happened between us, can you face him and pretend it didn't?"

At his blunt words, her skin flushed rosy, her reaction the ideal aid to win his argument. She dropped her gaze to the braided rug.

"It would be best if I slipped out the back, as if I were never here." He grabbed his hat and headed for the kitchen. "I'd rather you didn't tell him about me. Not yet."

"Why…? Wait! You can go out the front way," she insisted. "My father will be seeing to his horse first."

Her words came directly from behind, but Christopher paid them no heed. He knew from examining their plot of land prior to his initial arrival, a necessity for life as a fugitive, that the stable entrance was out of sight of the back door, the edge of the copse where he had tied his stallion a short distance farther, making it the safest way to depart. They entered the kitchen, and Nora looked up in surprise. He nodded and again thanked her for the meal, never slowing his rapid stride.

Erica followed him outdoors, putting a tentative hand to his sleeve. He turned to her in hurried question.

"I wish you didn't have to go like this and so soon. Just like last time."

"Maybe it's for the best and fate designed it this way. I meant what I said in there."

"So did I—and just maybe it was the Almighty who arranged for us to meet."

Shaking his head sadly, Christopher stared at her a little longer, wanting to carry with him what must be a last glimpse of her sweet, innocent face. "Don't wish for something you could never want, Erica. You'll only open yourself up to a world of pain and regret."

She could never love a man who was no more than a monster concealed beneath the trapping of a mask, and he would never be so selfish as to ask her to try.

With that gentle warning, he slipped away into the shadows of late evening.

Chapter 5

Erica took a deep breath to calm her nerves and returned to the parlor. She plinked a few keys on the piano as she waited, needing time to think and compose herself on the heels of Christopher's hasty departure. His cautionary farewell still puzzled her, doing the opposite of what he intended and making her even more intrigued about the man and what he was hiding.

She had spoken rather boldly on their short acquaintance, something for which she should feel penitent but didn't. Nor had she taken offense at his liberty either time he called her by her first name, as she'd done with Ralph. With Christopher, the stolen familiarity felt comfortable, pleasing. He had gently said her name again before he left, such intimacy not in keeping with his unspoken advice that she forget him. But forget him she would not.

Christopher was so unlike any man she'd known—the dark, vulnerable mystery of him, the rigid distance he maintained—and she wondered if his enigma was part of the appeal. Yet the tender kiss he instigated could not be called distant by any measure, and where before she would not have believed it, she was now certain he felt the same attraction she did.

The door opened. Her father strode inside, his husky build and calm blue eyes reassuring to see in his work-worn face, weathered dark by daily exposure to the sun.

Erica rose from the piano bench with a wide, welcoming smile and moved into her father's strong and swift embrace.

"It's so good to see you again, Papa. I was beginning to wonder."

He smiled. "I stopped at the jailhouse before coming home."

That came as no surprise.

"Ralph told me everything here is fine. You look well, even prettier and more grown up than I remember. Just how old are you now?"

She grinned. His mind might be shrewd enough to catch the wiliest criminal, but he was horrible when it came to the dates of memorable occasions.

"I turned twenty last month."

Her words had a strange effect on him. He sobered and grew distant, his mind clearly elsewhere. "Twenty? Already? I hadn't realized… Time goes so fast." He cleared his throat. "I imagine you'll soon be making a home of your own."

"One day I hope to. But I have no intention of doing so for some time."

"Is there someone I should know about?"

Immediately she thought of Christopher then flushed hot that she did.

"Has a certain deputy been coming to call?"

His light question made her ill at ease, and she wondered if Ralph had talked with him about such an impossible topic. "Papa, I'm sorry, but I have no interest in your deputy."

"That's a shame. You could do worse."

She sighed, wondering why she should settle for adequate when she desired the best. The best being true love, like he had shared with her mother.

"I really don't want to talk about this. Tell me of your trip. Did anything of interest occur?"

"We'll talk while I eat. I'm famished, and something smells good."

"It was, and there's plenty left. I'll get a plate for you."

Quickly she moved into the parlor ahead of him, relieved to see all evidence of Christopher's earlier presence gone. Nora had removed the three place settings from the table. Erica didn't feel comfortable hiding such things from her father, of course, but Christopher had asked her not to mention his visit, and this didn't seem the appropriate time to bring up her interest in a masked man living in the forest.

As her father ate, he filled her in on the events of his trip. Once he finished, Nora came in and brought him the rest of the cherry pie. His brows lifted.

"Pie yet? What's the occasion?"

Erica shared a quick warning glance with Nora, who shrugged at her father, answering with a vague smile: "Can't I make a cherry pie without there being a reason?"

"You can. But you rarely do."

"Papa, why don't you take that pie with you into the parlor, and I'll sing for you."

At Erica's quick suggestion, the mild suspicion left his eyes, and he nodded. "Now that's something I won't pass up. Even if I'm deaf to all those notes and can't make out the difference, I take pleasure in your singing."

Erica warmed to his words, glad for his company. He had forged a distance that became habitual after her mother died, with him spending long hours at the jailhouse and less time at home.

"I find it amazing that I'm able to sing at all, since neither you nor Mother could carry a tune," she teased but didn't get the amused smile or witty retort she expected. Instead, her father's brow wrinkled, his eyes almost pained.

"Never mind," she urged, worried and curious as to why he was behaving so strangely. "Come into the parlor and relax, Papa."

She played for him the song she earlier played for Christopher, the memory of what then followed causing her heart to race faster than her fingers on the keys. Knowing her face must be glowing like the rhododendrons that bloomed outside, and for the first time seeing the wisdom of Christopher's swift departure—had he also been seated on the divan she doubted she would have been able to pretend those moments away—Erica gave a mini performance. She played until she had again composed herself and could face her father.

Foolishness, perhaps, since she and Christopher had done nothing wrong. But his was the first kiss she'd ever received, and it had affected her deeply, making her feel both warm and soft inside, and entirely like a woman.

She turned on the bench and noticed she wasn't the only one lost to memories. Her father sat staring, and though he looked straight at her, she sensed that he didn't see her. His pie sat barely touched.

"Papa?"

He blinked then shook his head as if not wishing to speak. His gaze dropped to his plate.

She left the piano and approached him in mounting alarm. "You don't look well. Are you feeling all right? Is there anything I can get you?"

"Sit down, Erica," he said wearily. "It's time we had a talk."

The crackling fire leaped toward the winter night sky, a greedy monster hell-bent on destruction, its yellow teeth consuming everything in its path.

Christopher stared in horror at the sight of his best friend's home ablaze. A scream of pain and terror reverberated from somewhere inside.

Without thought to his own safety, Christopher raced forward and broke through the door. Dark smoke obscured his vision as the intense inferno ate through three walls of the parlor. He coughed, his eyes stinging and watering from the fumes. Repeatedly he called out but heard no reply. Seeing no one downstairs, he raised his arm up in front of his face as a vain shield and hurried upstairs. The bed was engulfed in flames, its occupant beyond saving.

A roar and crack of breaking timbers sounded from outside the room. Christopher fled, sensing he had little time before the entire place would collapse. He rushed downstairs and looked up to see a plank of burning wood careening toward him. The blow slammed him on the shoulder, the fire searing his face.

He howled in pain, blindly striking out with his other hand, and fell to his knees. Suddenly his hand met with the grasp of another, and he felt those hands slap out the fire from his hair and shirt, then himself

being pulled and lifted, carried away from scorch-
ing heat and strangling smoke into cold night air.
He blacked out from the agonizing pain.

With a shock, Christopher woke and sat up in his bed-roll.

Cold sweat trickled down his heated face and dripped between his shoulders. He snapped away the buckskin mask Chester's mother had dyed light black for a worthy disguise in the night, when he traveled, his fingers finding the disgusting evidence that it had not all been a dream. Scars of warped skin he could barely feel on the surface ached beneath from where his face had been pressed to the ground in sleep.

He should have died, but Chester, the oxlike mute who kept the stables, saved him. As a boy, Christopher and the other children wrongly thought his mother, a reclusive old woman, was a witch. After the fire, with her many herbs and remedies, she had brought him from the brink of death, though it took weeks before he mended well enough to leave his sickbed. His shoulder where the beam had hit him and his upper back were also burned, his ability to move limited at first. New skin had formed as grotesque scars. She called it a miracle from God that he was alive and that Chester found him in time to beat out the flames before they could completely burn his skin away. Bitter upon seeing the damage, Christopher said that God had not saved him but instead had made him into a monster. The rest of his life shortly crumbled to dust once he learned the horrid truth of what led to the fire and its tragic results.

The distant whinny of a horse broke through his bitter musings. Instantly alert, he swiftly replaced his mask, slipped his suspenders back over his shoulders, and pulled his boots and jacket on, buckling his gun belt around him. Grabbing his rifle, he silently crept to the edge of the forest.

The sound of a woman's soft weeping startled him. He hurried toward the break in the trees, having no doubt who he would find there.

The moon, hanging directly above in a starlit sky, shone softly down on Erica, sitting at the top of the hill, her hair in wild disarray all around her. Christopher hurried up the path, for once giving no caution to silence. At the rustle of his footsteps, Erica grabbed her Derringer, her upper body twisting around in his direction.

"It's only me," he said calmly then watched both her gun and head lower.

He approached in concern.

"Are you hurt?" He crouched beside her, setting his rifle down, and grabbed her shoulders, trying to see her face. She shook her head, still not looking at him as she tucked her weapon inside her boot.

"You're shaking like a leaf." The summer evening was cool, and he wondered how long she'd been outdoors. He helped her to her feet and removed his jacket, wrapping it around her. Her body still shivered, and he drew her close. She needed warmth, though by her behavior he wondered if she shook from more than the night air.

His heart torn, he hesitated at the notion of what he was about to do but felt he had no choice. She was dangerous to his continued safety, her father the leading law official who had just returned from Christopher's home state and surely would have found out about him—but he couldn't leave her where she was, alone and distraught.

"Come. You need a fire to get you warm."

She offered no question or refusal, waiting as he untied her mare and grabbed his rifle then led them both deeper into the forest to the seclusion of his camp.

He tied her horse near his and hurried to add to the fire. Once the flames crackled in a low blaze of warmth, Christopher returned to where Erica still stood, motionless, in a clear state of shock. Alarmed by her unresponsive behavior and whatever calamity had brought her to such a state, he led her by the hand, gently helping her to sit. She seemed as fragile as a child.

Throwing out what bitter dregs of coffee remained in the pot, he filled it with fresh beans and water and set the container on the rocks over the fire.

She had not once looked away from the flames, though he doubted she really saw them.

"Erica… ?" He sank to the ground beside her. "Tell me, angel, what's wrong?" The endearment came without thought but under the circumstances didn't seem misplaced.

She shivered a little and closed her eyes. A tear seeped beneath her dark, wet lashes and rolled down her cheek.

His heart twisting at the sight, Christopher wrapped his arm around her back, drawing her close. She laid her head in the crook of his neck, her soft crown of curls pressed against his jaw. They sat like that for some time in silence, watching the fire, while a dozen horrific possibilities slithered through Christopher's mind.

"I'm sorry," she whispered at last. "I don't mean always to be a burden and get in the way. I really had no clear thought of coming here. I just suddenly found myself at the hill. I often go there, even before you came."

"Why did you leave?" he asked, chagrined that she would think of herself as unwanted and feel the need to make excuses for her presence, though he had given her little reason to feel otherwise.

"I needed to get away from the house… I learned something about myself tonight, my heritage…" She took in a fractured breath, and he protectively tightened his hold.

He waited for her to go on. An owl hooted in the distance. The horses softly whickered while the flames slowly crackled. Erica's body stilled its trembling, but Christopher didn't release her from his hold.

"My father said he and Mother discussed it after I was born and agreed to tell me when I was twenty," she finally said. "They're not my parents…or, they are, but… Oh, it's all just so *wrong*…" She groaned and took a deep breath before continuing. "The woman who bore me was a former opera singer they met on the Oregon Trail. She died of a fever two months after I was born. My father didn't want me. Said he had no use for an infant and gave me to the Chandlers then headed for California."

Tears clenched her voice, which had gone soft and sad and angry. He lifted his other hand to stroke her curls in what little comfort he could offer.

"It all makes sense, what never did before. My musical talent, why I never had brothers and sisters—I was told tonight that the woman I knew as my mother was barren—and the man I understood to be my father always distanced himself from me after she died. He didn't want me either, not with her gone."

Where before Erica was silent, now she seemed unable to restrain the words that wounded her, and they came out fast and furious. Christopher wished he knew what to say to help, but having never met her father he could only go by what she'd told him.

"Did he say that?" he asked quietly.

"No. But that must be the reason. He tolerated my presence while she was alive, but afterward he found excuses to stay away from home, from *me*." She shook her head against him. "I feel hurt and betrayed by those who

I thought loved me. My world feels as if it's caved in—everything I thought true is false—my entire life a lie, and I can't push away the pieces to struggle up and breathe. Even *Nora* knew! She came over on the same wagon train."

Christopher understood about pain and betrayal and being cast aside as unwanted. He could write a whole book on the subject, but his bitter tragedy she didn't need to hear, not that he would ever tell it.

"It seems to me," he began after a lengthy span of silence fraught by her tears that came just as quiet and made a slow, pitiful roll to her tight jaw, "that you have no need for concern with regard to his feelings for you."

At his low words, he felt her stiffen against him.

"Any man who buys his daughter so fine a piano and arranges to have it brought all the way to Washington seems more than just tolerant. And it's clear Nora dotes on you. I would say that you're blessed to have such people to call family. Not everyone is so fortunate."

At first he thought she might take offense at his mild reminder, as her shoulders firmed even more. Then the tension eased, and she gave a short nod.

"You're right, I suppose. I just… I can't go back there."

He turned his head sharply to look at her. She continued staring at the fire.

"Where will you go?"

For a moment she didn't speak. "Can I stay with you?"

Her cheeks grew flushed in the glow of the flames, and his eyes widened at what she proposed. That was all he needed, to have her lawman father round up a search party and find her sleeping in his camp. The alarming idea spurred another.

"Does anyone know you left?"

She shook her head. "After he told me, I went to my room. Nora came to my door and tried to speak through it, but I didn't want to hear what she had to say and told her I wished to be left alone. I felt numb but angry. It was too much, too soon. My behavior might seem foolish and childish, but it *hurt* to hear those things. To learn that my parents were not who I'd always thought them to be and what kind of man my true father was—and how badly he treated everyone. I was told that tonight, too—and, well, I had to get away. I really don't know where I belong anymore. I just know I don't want to go back there. It's the last place I wish to be!"

Christopher swallowed hard, trying to think over the pounding in his ears that echoed the hammering of his heart. "I understand, and I really am sorry you had a bad time of it. I'm sorry you got hurt. But you can't stay here with me. I'm sure if you think on it, you'll understand why."

She frowned and pulled away, sitting forward. "I only thought to make a bed on the other side of the fire. I wasn't implying…"

"I never thought you were," he assured when she broke off, flustered.

This had a lot more to do with other concerns than just her father and the danger he posed to Christopher. The strong urge to feel her soft lips against his had led him to give in to his desire to kiss Erica while Nora was in the next room. His kiss had been impulsive, warm and innocent, but a liberty taken all the same. Alone together, in a dark forest, he wasn't about to test the beckoning hand of temptation a second time.

He covered the awkward moment by pouring coffee into his one tin mug and handing it to Erica. She took it between her hands with quiet thanks and blew at the steam. Another lapse of silence passed as she took several sips.

"Do you wish he would have kept the truth from you and never told you?" Christopher asked at last.

"When you put it like that…" She sighed. "No, I suppose not. It's better knowing the truth, even though it hurts, than it is continuing in a lie. Which is what I feel my life has been up until this point."

"Were you unhappy growing up there?"

She thought about that. "No. I had everything I wanted as a child. I did feel lonely a lot of the time after Mother died. Nora and Papa were always busy, but I learned to cope." She paused in recollection then shrugged. "He's not always distant. Sometimes I get the feeling he just doesn't know how to talk to me. Tonight was the first time in a long time he has." She grew sullen again and drank more of her coffee.

He nodded. "That makes sense. Sometimes I don't know how to talk to you—not in a way that'll make you listen."

She looked at him then, a smile teasing her lips at his light comment that he phrased in such a way to pull her out of her bleak mood. "You're doing a good job of it right now. Which begs the question—why do you hide alone in a forest? Why don't you ever go into town? No one has even heard of you."

Her curious words triggered his alarm. "You've talked about me to others?"

A betraying flush tinged her skin. "I didn't come right out and ask, no, but I did ask around about any strangers anyone might have recently met."

He frowned and stood. "It's time you went home."

"Please don't be angry, Christopher. I didn't give your location away. I didn't even know it before tonight."

Hearing her say his name so softly made him go warm inside. It strengthened his resolve.

"You need to leave," he insisted quietly.

Erica rose to her feet. "Can I at least finish my coffee?"

"It's best if you go now."

She frowned, clearly hurt by his sudden curt distance, but he only turned his back on her and moved toward her horse. Untying the rope, he brought the mare to her.

He escorted her through the break in the trees, accompanying her up the path to the top of the hill. "I trust you can take it from here?" he asked, his words an echo of the first day they met.

She nodded and opened her mouth to speak then closed it for a moment before breaking the silence. "Thank you for your trouble," she said quietly. She slid his jacket from her shoulders, handing it to him.

Her body no longer shivered, but she looked lost, forlorn, and distraught, and it was all Christopher could do not to give in to her request to stay. All he could do not to give in to the desire to pull her back into his arms. He watched as she mounted, then he shrugged into his jacket and hurried back to camp, mounting his own horse. The hide against his shirt felt warmer from the heat of her body and held the faintest scent of rose water, further muddling his senses.

Foolishly wishing for what he could never have for the entirety of the nighttime ride, Christopher caught up to the sight of Erica and followed at a distance, so as to remain undetected. He wanted to make sure she arrived home safely, that she arrived home at all. From the little he knew of Erica, in her present state of mind he wouldn't put it past her to do something as foolhardy as find a quiet spot in the forest and make her own camp. And wild animals roamed these forests at night. He had confronted the danger many times.

To his distress, his feelings for the gentle and exasperating Erica had matured beyond mere concern. Nothing could ever come of them, of course. There were too many obstacles to allow for a close relationship. Even friendship remained out of the question.

He had been harsh with her, even cruel, necessary behavior to make her go and discourage her from ever coming in search of him again. He didn't suspect her curiosity to be malicious with the intent to do him harm; she seemed innocent enough. But he wished that she hadn't made inquiries in town.

The Chandler's frame house rose into view, and Christopher reined to a stop and waited. Not until she led her mare to the stable then, minutes later, slipped through the back door from which he exited hours before did he turn his horse back to camp.

The following day his mild viewpoint of her integrity changed and hardened as, from his hiding place, Christopher watched in hurt and angry disbelief while Erica walked with his enemy down the town's main street. Both were in deep discussion and clearly more than passing acquaintances—evident by that touch on the arm. He growled beneath his breath upon seeing it.

How long had they known each other? Did she spy for him? Is that why she'd sought him out time after time?

Christopher narrowly watched them part on a cordial note. His resentment rose yet another notch when, from his concealment in the shadows, he overheard two men walk by in snide discussion:

"...her talk of a masked stranger, did she really think that creating a story would incite the boss's interest?"

"With the likes of Miss Chandler, who knows, Lou? She thinks that because her father is the law that gives her license to do as she pleases."

"Think there's any truth to her claim?"

The man guffawed. "The same woman who as a child made up fictional characters and insisted they were real? Not likely. She'll do anything for a place at *The Chronicle*, not that she'll ever get it…"

The men walked out of the range of his hearing, leaving Christopher in a state of numb shock and once again feeling betrayed.

Chapter 6

The morning after her world toppled on its axis dawned no brighter for Erica.

She had spent a restless night, tossing and turning in the covers. Angry with the world and all who resided in it, she remained silent when Nora served her breakfast. Afterward, hardly knowing what she ate, Erica announced she would be going to town and left to saddle Ginger.

She had been foolish to go to that hill, even more so to ask Christopher if she could stay. In her shock and pain she hadn't been thinking clearly to make such an indecent request. Oddly, she felt even more vexed with Christopher that he *was* a gentleman and not the rogue she'd first thought, instead seeking to protect her reputation. But if he *had* agreed to let her stay, she might not think so highly of his character at this moment—and then could stop thinking of him at all!

The memory of the previous night carried her halfway to town. She didn't know if it was due to the vibrant aromas of the pines and firs after a brief morning shower and the sunlit surroundings all around her, the droplets of water caught on green-needled boughs, the blades of grass sparkling like thousands of tiny iridescent jewels, but a measure of peace slowly stole into her heart and chased away the bitterness.

The sorrow and remorse that had shown in her father's eyes, the tired expression on his swarthy face, all of it now tugged at her heart. She wanted to harden herself to his pain—hadn't he brought it on himself by his decision to allow her to believe a lie?—but found that she could not be so callous. The mother who raised her taught her the importance of forgiveness, and Nora had continued the teaching. A lifetime of the need for mercy consistently ingrained within Erica was difficult to toss aside. The truth still hurt deeply, but finding blame failed to matter. With regard to Erica, God only looked at what composed her heart. She had been taught that precept as a small child. And to her chagrin, she had behaved like one last night, throwing a fit of temper then rushing off to hide in her room, later slipping away and riding out into the darkness.

She still had questions and knew the only way to satisfy them was to breach this new gap between herself and her father. To go forward rather than flounder in a past new to her, one she couldn't possibly begin to understand on her own.

But those in town had other plans for her morning's activity.

Once she arrived, it seemed everyone she knew and caught sight of within a twenty-yard radius wished to converse. Shamus came up to her and asked if all was well since he'd re-shod Ginger, assuring if it wasn't, his young nephew, the true culprit, had returned his tools. Mr. Barker from the lumber mill approached in clear pain and asked Shamus to pull a sore tooth. No sooner had the two men left than Mrs. Pemberley, with four-year-old Anna clinging to her mother's hand, hurried up to speak with Erica about performing at a benefit to help supply the church with real songbooks. Giving her assurance that she would sing, at last Erica excused herself from the talkative woman, smiled at the shy Anna, and moved toward the jailhouse.

Before she could enter, Ralph stepped outside.

She curbed an impatient groan. "Good morning, deputy. I was hoping to speak with my father."

Ralph stopped her, briefly putting his hand to her arm before she could walk through the door. "He's not here. He went to the logging camp but should be back soon." He seemed nervous, pushing up the brim of his hat only to tug it back down a few seconds later. "As a matter of fact, there's something I need to speak with you about, Miss Erica. Will you walk with me?"

Not failing to notice his small concession to formality, she nodded, again finding it strange that she'd felt no such reluctance in allowing Christopher the privilege. Perhaps because he was always so intent on pushing her away.

"I don't know if your pa told you, but I'm leaving town at the end of this month."

"Oh. Visiting relations?"

"Something like that. My mother has been tending the farm by herself since my brother left and my sister recently married. It's too much for a woman her age."

"So you'll be going for a visit to help?"

"Actually, I plan on staying."

Erica regarded him with surprise. He had barely been in town six months.

She smiled at him kindly. Ralph might be overbearing, but deep down his heart was golden, and she had no wish to be cruel.

"Your presence will be missed. My father never had such a good deputy; he's told me so before," she added hastily, not failing to notice the strange spark that lit his eyes with the emergence of her first words.

He hesitated, coming to a stop and turning toward her. "The parcel of land that my family's farm sits on is rich. It's a sweet slice, a hundred acres. I think you'd like the Willamette Valley…"

Alarms went off inside her. Merciful heavens, was he about to propose—and here? In the middle of a busy street? By his intent, hopeful manner, she realized that was exactly what he planned!

"Oh, I could never leave my home." Her words came politely soft and desperately quick. "This is where I belong." A strange thing to say when the previous night she had felt so estranged from it. But once she spoke the words, she felt the grain of their truth.

The hope in Ralph's eyes faded. "Do you think you could ever change your mind, given the right incentive?"

The right incentive would consist of love. If she cared about a man with her entire heart, only then might she reconsider. Of course, Erica didn't tell *him* that, worried he might then try to woo her mercilessly in the hope of gaining her deep affection in these next two weeks before his departure.

"I'm not like you, deputy. I may have been born on the trail in the middle of nowhere, but that's as far as my wandering spirit goes. Barretts Grove will always be my home." She wondered if her feelings of clinging to a place familiar to her stemmed from some innate knowledge previously closed to her awareness that she'd been an orphan. Perhaps not an orphan in the purest sense—as far as anyone knew, she still had a father. He just didn't want her. But to Erica that amounted to the same thing.

"I see." Ralph nodded. "Well, I reckon that's that, then."

She couldn't help but notice his injured feelings in the sudden slump of his shoulders and the hasty downward tilt of his hat, and she laid a gentle hand upon his sleeve.

"If I don't see you again before you go, I want to wish you the very best, Ralph." Under the circumstances, she conceded to the informality, no longer worried he might get the wrong impression. "You've been a good friend, to me and my father."

"It's been a pleasure knowing you, Miss Erica." He gave her a calm smile, and while it didn't come across as entirely genuine, he didn't seem too distraught. She felt assured he would soon get over whatever affection he felt. "I should be going. I have business to tend to."

"Of course."

She watched him go for a moment before turning back the way she'd come, toward the jailhouse. At the sight of Jake Millstone stepping off the boardwalk across the street and making a direct course for where she stood, she groaned and wryly wondered if she was being punished for her bad behavior the previous evening.

"Good day, Miss Chandler. I was hoping to run into you again soon."

"Mr. Millstone." She inclined her head in a polite nod. "You wished to speak with me?"

"Yes, I do. I have plans to buy out Mr. Boswell, and I hear you are quite the songbird, which comes as little surprise. Your speaking voice is quite lovely."

His charisma grated on nerves already frayed, but his insinuation caused her blood to boil. "You bought the saloon, and now you wish for me to come work there?"

He chuckled nervously. "Not if you don't wish to. Just

to come by for a song now and then. You make it sound so sordid."

"I call it what it is." As a child, curiosity had led her to peek between slats of the swinging doors. She had gaped at the sight of the garishly painted women in brilliant costume, shamelessly exposing black stockings as they sang bawdy tunes.

"Never mind. I didn't intend to insult you." He laid his hand lightly on her sleeve. "I only wished to hear you sing."

Erica calmed, somewhat pacified by the regret in his eyes, and smoothly pulled her arm out of his reach.

"I often sing at church meetings. You're welcome to attend them. I need to go now. Good day, Mr. Millstone."

Erica nodded politely in farewell and continued toward the jailhouse, relieved when he didn't follow.

She realized that her own state of affairs had led her to react more violently than she normally would have. Her birth father was a ruthless gambler and who knew what else. Jake's unknowing invitation only added another layer of grime to how dirty she felt just from what she'd learned of the man who'd sired her. For the first time, she felt extremely grateful that the Chandlers had taken her in, whatever their reason for lying to her all these years.

More determined than ever to mend things with her father, Erica walked into the jailhouse to wait for him. Restless, she leisurely strolled around the room, grateful the cells were empty so as not to be overheard, then found herself at his desk, where she began to straighten clutter. Books, papers, and a half-eaten browned apple rested on a stack. Disposing of it, she rubbed her hands on her skirts and looked at the three bulletins on the wall. A new poster had appeared since her last visit.

Her heart froze in shock then slowly began to pound. She moved closer, hardly daring to believe what her eyes told her was true, praying that it was all some horrible mistake…

She had seen that strong, lean jaw, those chiseled, full lips with the dimple beside them, the slight cleft in the chin…and those intense eyes that, even from a black-and-white drawing, still mesmerized her and burned into her soul.

Christopher's striking, unmasked face stared at her from the wanted poster, easily recognizable with those features she had seen below the covering of dark leather.

Her stunned gaze dropped, and she inhaled a pained breath as the price for his capture—in the largest type at the very bottom—screamed out from the poster.

The bounty on his head was more than she'd seen in her life, more than her father probably made in a year. A $500 reward in gold coin…

She read the brief caption:

Christopher Duvall
Wanted—Dead or Alive
For Arson, Theft, Murder

Murder…

Erica pressed a hand to the wall to keep her balance, feeling the blood drain from her head. Of all crimes, murder was the most reprehensible in her eyes. Money could be given back. Buildings could be rebuilt. But a human life, once taken, could never be restored.

"Oh, Christopher…why?" Tears burned her eyes, and she backed away, pushing her fist to her mouth and biting down hard on her finger so as not to scream or weep or moan with anguish.

In the turbulent silence, she stared at the poster, knowing she was duty bound as a law-abiding citizen to tell her father, to turn Christopher over to his authority. But…she couldn't! This had to be some horrible, grievous, tragic error. That could happen. It was possible…only a lie.

So many lies…

Not Christopher.

No, it wasn't possible.

Erica moaned and covered her mouth with her palm. No matter how pretty a picture her life had been or how honorable a deed done by the Chandlers in taking her as their own, her existence was based on a lie…. Christopher had remained silent about his past, with good reason, but to her knowledge, he had never lied when he could have….

Unless omission was a lie.

And this was indeed real.

Erica felt so confused as she stared at the accusation, at the handsome face of the man who had become so familiar to her, so…cherished. And she suddenly panicked that someone might come inside and find her on the verge of hysteria.

Quickly she left the jailhouse.

She could stand no more deceit.

Before she could decide what should be done about this, she must know the truth.

She pushed Ginger into a hard gallop once she'd left town. At the hill, she took the path into the forest. She had only been to his camp once, but she had an uncanny sense for recalling places and directions, and the trail they made was still visible from last night.

Praying none of this was real, that it was all some dreadful mistake, Erica hurried through the trees, out of breath by the time she reached his campsite.

The area had been deserted, the remains of a campfire the only proof he'd ever been near.

* * *

In the stillness of the night, an angel's voice reached inside Christopher's heart, chasing away shadows of cloying darkness that had long made its home there.

How could she sing with such beauty, her voice so pure and undefiled, and sing such words of conviction and comfort in a God who watched over his own, when it had been *she* who betrayed his trust?

Torn between the familiar bitterness and a beckoning hope, Christopher approached the window and blinked away moisture that had gathered in his eyes at the sweetness of her hymn.

It had been foolish to stay, but he couldn't leave these forests of Washington. Not yet. Not when he was so close to his goal. Exactly what led him back to the Chandler's land, he couldn't name, but the moment he heard the faint strains of Erica's voice in the air, so rich and full of a sadness never there before, he'd been helplessly drawn back to the spot where he stood days ago.

She couldn't see him where he watched, her back to him as she sat at the piano and played. The cascade of her long curls shone in the lamplight. Her slight body gracefully moved from side to side as she put her heart into her music and played with her soul, her appearance and voice reminding him of angels and heaven and all things worthy and perfect. In a daze, he continued to listen, a flicker lighting within him for what he'd lost, for the God he had turned his back to in anger, the God that he felt had unjustly abandoned him to a living hell upon the earth.

In Erica's voice there was refreshment. Hope. Peace. How could someone sing like that and shield a heart so wicked? How could she do what she'd done for him, inviting him to sup at her table, seeming to care for his welfare—then go behind his back and consort with his enemy with the intent to harm? Something didn't add up. She hated deceit, traumatized when she learned the truth of her birth and that her lineage had been kept from her. He remembered her own pain at the feeling of being betrayed.

Had he misjudged her motives? Was it possible she had no idea that the man she'd been speaking with so cordially days ago was Christopher's adversary, whose seeming kindness and sometimes quiet attitude fooled many? Had it all been a case of bizarre happenstance?

Even if she wasn't blameworthy in that regard, there was still her desire to obtain a job at the town's newspaper. Christopher could think of no other reason for her wishing to spend time with him without it being connected to that goal—but suddenly he wanted to know. The desire for the truth burned inside, and he almost stepped forward.

Erica stopped playing and sat very still. Christopher inhaled a slow breath, unable to take his eyes from her. Swiftly she turned to look out the open window, her eyes widening in surprise as they met his.

For several breathless seconds he could not move, rooted to the spot.

She jumped off the bench and hurried for the door.

Shaking the fog from his brain, he pushed away from the wall and sped toward the trees. The soft thuds of running footsteps behind attested to her whereabouts.

"Wait!" she cried out. *"Oh, please...wait!"*

The desperation in her voice, laced with hope bound in pain, acted like ropes of restraint tossed around him, holding him back. He stopped running at the edge of the forest, caught by her plea, suddenly drained of the will to escape her, like a tired stallion who had run long and hard, lassoed by a slip of a girl who could bring about his untimely demise. He could easily evade her and conceal himself where she would never find him, his stride much faster than hers, his ability to blend into shadows well learned, but he realized he didn't want to. He was tired of running, weary of hiding, and his deprived heart decided his fate for him.

Fool.

He closed his mind to his lack of sense and stood silent.

Her skirts rustled as she came up close behind, breathless, the warmth of her hand tentatively resting on his shoulder.

His own breath coming fast, Christopher did not dare turn around.

Chapter 7

Beneath her hand, the muscles of his back stiffened.

Erica looked with some surprise at the outline of her pale fingers boldly pressed against his jacket. Even standing as still as he was, he exuded the impression of strength. Being this close after days of wondering if she would ever see him again, and touching him, proof he was really there, made her feel weak, lightheaded…

He still had not moved to look at her.

Coming to a sudden awareness of the danger, Erica pulled her hand away from his shoulder and glanced toward the house, hoping Nora remained immersed in her cleaning but not willing to take a chance. She issued a silent prayer of relief that her father was still in town.

She moved in front of Christopher and boldly grabbed his arm. "Come. We can't talk here."

Hurriedly she drew him with her a short distance past

the trees, so she could keep an eye on the house but no one could see them or hear their conversation.

She released his arm. He still had not spoken. With the moon partly shrouded by the thick boughs above, most of his face remained in shadow, a slight gleam all that showed of his eyes behind the mask, reflecting the distant moonlight.

She should be frightened after what she had learned, nervous, at the very least awkward, but she felt nothing but a sense of timeliness to be in his company. A settled peace even while she was concerned, a sweet warmth even while he remained so distant. It had been almost a week since they last parted, and despite the gravity of the situation, Erica felt so thankful to be near him again. Yet for all that, her feelings didn't change facts, and she needed to hear the truth, no matter how difficult it would be.

"I know your secret," she began. "That you're wanted for murder. Arson. Theft. I saw the wanted poster at the jailhouse with your face."

A sharp inhalation of breath was his only sign of emotion. He didn't move a muscle.

"So now you're going to turn me in?"

Despite the low, dead tone to his words, a warm shiver went through her to hear his voice again. "Before I answer, I want to hear your story. Did…did you really do those things?"

"Would you believe me if I said no?"

"I've never caught you in a lie. You've barely said much at all."

He snorted a self-derisive laugh and took a few steps away. "Can you blame me for keeping quiet, knowing what you now do?" He turned toward her again. "And knowing what I know about you?"

"What do you mean?" She shook her head in confusion. "What do you know?"

"That you're striving to be a journalist." He hissed the words. "And you're looking for a juicy story to land you the position."

She sucked in a breath. "Who told you that?"

"Doesn't matter. Is it true?"

At the angry accusation in his voice, she deeply regretted her initial idea to investigate him.

"Yes."

"And is that the reason you were always snooping around, meddling in my affairs?" he asked, not mincing words. "Because you wanted *me* to be that story?"

She knew that honesty was golden, but sometimes, like now, it was so tempting to lie.

But temptation demanded so much, the least of which were her scruples. It was best to close the door on its lure before it could cause even more harm. She had learned through her own troubles that a smooth lie dug an even deeper well of heartache than the hard, cold truth could ever manage.

"Yes, at first," she admitted quietly. "But all that's changed."

He closed the distance between them. "How so? Did you wake up one morning and give up the idea to be a writer?"

Skepticism lay heavy in his tone, and she prayed for words to which he would be receptive.

"I didn't know you then, Christopher. You were just a masked stranger who came out of nowhere. I didn't think there would be any harm in writing about you. I thought afterward, when I showed you the article, you might even be pleased. That is, until the other day..."

"After you saw the wanted poster with the bounty on my head." He nodded curtly. "And I assume you hurried to tell your father? Tell me, Erica, is a search party hunting me out even now? Are your father and his deputy scouring those woods?"

Beneath the sarcastic bent of his low words, she heard a wealth of pain.

"I didn't tell him anything. I didn't wait for his return. I mounted my horse and rode home. And I haven't told him since. He knows nothing about you."

Short, tense seconds elapsed.

"You didn't tell him?" He sounded puzzled. "Why not?"

"After what happened, with me, I've come to realize that my parents withheld the truth to protect me and give me a happy childhood. They thought they were doing the best thing, I suppose. While I still don't think omission is always right, in this case I decided to withhold the truth, at least for now. I want to hear your story first."

"So you can write it up for an article in *The Chronicle*?" He took a few angry steps away.

Erica winced at his accusatory words, however well deserved his censure. She watched him where he remained with his back to her, his head bowed.

"I'm *not* writing that story, Christopher. I would never do anything to hurt you. I hope you can believe that. I acted in ignorance. I didn't see anything wrong with hunting up a story, and you were a character of interest. Now I realize that's an understatement and revealing your identity could get you killed. And I *would never* make that happen. I couldn't live with myself."

"You believe I'm innocent?"

"I want to…but how would I honestly know? I don't know your story, so I can't form an opinion." She took a careful step his way. "But if I were to judge based on character alone, I would have to say there's been some mistake. Unless it was in self-defense, I can't picture you taking anyone's life in cold blood."

"Why?"

"Why?" She shook her head in confusion at his choked whisper. "You're just not like that. I know we've only known each other nearly three weeks, but in that time, you've come to my aid—even saved my life since I don't know what would have become of me if I'd been unable to make it up that hill before nightfall. You expressed concern that I might get lost after I followed you, and when I needed a shoulder to cry on, you were there." Her voice became gentle with the desire to encourage. "I just don't see you being a dangerous outlaw. Tell me I'm not wrong."

He turned sideways, moving his head to look in her direction. "You would believe me if I did?"

It was the second time he had asked. "Why do you have such a hard time thinking that I would?"

He let out a small, self-deprecating laugh. "My friends didn't believe me. My *grandfather* didn't believe me." He gave a little shake of his head. "Even the girl who'd been my sweetheart for two years and who said she would always love me wanted nothing more to do with me after what happened."

Erica felt a sharp twinge in the center of her chest at his mention of a girl.

"All of them turned on me; the whole town was after me." Again he shook his head as if unable to understand. "I had everything I could want—my future mapped out, even had a little plot of land where I was planning to build a cabin. What would I want with all that money? Wealth only brings trouble; I saw that firsthand."

His words came, harsh, bitter, a dam unstopped and running freely now that he'd begun, as if he spoke not to her but argued with an unseen prosecutor.

"Yes! I was there that night—but I never set out to kill anyone. Just the opposite, little good it did." He tore his hat off and slapped it against his leg. "Do you have any idea what it's like to wake up one morning and learn you're wanted for some of the most heinous crimes known to man, that overnight you've become an outcast to society? It's like the end of the world came early…." He shook his head. "Their minds had been poisoned against me. Lies, vicious lies spread not to sully my character—oh, no. That would have been too easy. He wanted to completely destroy me. But *why*?" He looked her way as if she could give him an answer, though she had trouble trying to decipher his fervent question. "I followed the Good Book, went to church meetings, tried to be a good man. Why did God turn on me like this and let that scoundrel go free?"

Erica took in a slow breath. His furious words did little to persuade her of his innocence. Despite his mention of being a God-fearing man, his indistinct rant seemed to cage him within a greater wall of guilt. That his loved ones would reject him confused her. But she didn't believe in judging a man based on what those nameless others said. She wanted to hear all of his story.

"Maybe you should start from the beginning," she suggested quietly.

He gave another humorless laugh and slowly shook his head. "I'm not going about this very well, am I?"

"Actually…no. If you were in a courtroom and that's your defense, I don't think you should take the witness stand. Guilty or not, the judge and jury would condemn you on the spot."

He groaned. "I must be going mad. What am I doing telling you this? Your father's *the sheriff*!"

"I had hoped that maybe you felt you could trust me, though I've done little to deserve it." She calmly approached him. "You helped me so much the other night, just being there to listen while I poured out my troubles to you. Now I want to help, if I can. Please. Forget about my father for the moment. Tell me your story."

Christopher drew in a deep breath to calm himself. Never had he gone off like that, losing his composure so quickly. Never had he told so much of his wretched life to anyone. He had been too bitter with his fate to say much to Chester's mom during his recovery, and to the dear half-blind elderly woman, Mrs. Waterbury, he'd told only the barest portion.

He shouldn't trust Erica, though he wanted to believe her sincere admission that she'd given up writing the story. But her father was the top lawman in these parts, the man who could sign Christopher's death warrant, for crying out loud. And he'd seen her in town with his *enemy*, the scoundrel who'd done him the most harm and would soon pay for every one of his foul, black sins.

So *why* was he doing this?

In the darkness, her face appeared hazy, none of her delicate features clear. But her voice had been gentle, her manner sympathetic, and earlier when she'd caught him and moved to confront him, the light from the window had reflected in her tear-bright eyes. There he had glimpsed concern, even what looked like relief, and he wondered if she could actually be *glad* that he'd come tonight, especially after having seen the wanted poster in her father's jailhouse. The artist must be highly skilled to have sketched his image without the mask and have her recognize him. Save for a very few, no one knew what he now looked like or that he wore a covering over his face.

He studied her dim silhouette in confusion. Her desire to seek him out made no sense—that she would bring him to this dark spot in the woods, alone, after having seen a list of his alleged crimes.

Just as it made no sense that the desire to tell her of that night grew the longer he waited.

He closed his eyes. "It's not a pretty story. Not something you would want to hear."

He realized that he was stalling with his flimsy excuse, as tough as he knew Erica to be, but was amazed to hear her chuckle in amusement, even more astonished that she didn't seem the least bit anxious or fearful to be with him. She seemed truly at ease in his presence, and she hadn't yet heard his story. He still couldn't believe that she had chased him down to speak with him, with no real knowledge of his innocence or guilt. What if he *were* a murderer, out to do her harm for what she now knew?

Admiration of her courage fought with annoyance and a hint of alarm at her recklessness. He tried to recall if there was a full moon. When Christopher was a boy, his grandfather told him that a full moon sometimes made people do the most bizarre things, things they wouldn't normally do. He could believe it. There had been a full moon that night, too.

"I'm the sheriff's daughter," she said, her voice light. "I assure you, any delicate sensibilities I had were roughened at the edges a long time ago."

He voiced his curiosity. "I guess that makes sense, for you to be out here with me, alone at night, when I'm virtually a stranger."

"I trust you, Christopher. You would never harm me; I know that. And I don't think of you as a stranger, not anymore. I consider you…a friend."

Her voice was both shy and reassuring, and he shook his head a little in disbelief that she actually had come to feel that way about him. When was the last time he'd had a friend to talk to, someone with whom to share?

"It's a long story." He motioned to a log, stripped of most of its limbs. "Let's sit there."

He heard his horse softly whicker and noted its dark outline. At least he could make a quick getaway if needed. Her father could return any moment.

Once they were seated on the low trunk, Christopher stretched his long legs out before him, crossing them at the ankles. He gripped the log on either side while grimly staring at his boot tips. Erica sat quietly beside him and waited as he mulled over what to relay and what to omit. He couldn't tell her everything, only those things he felt she needed to know.

"I lived with my grandfather, as I told you. I enjoyed music and books, not your typical boyhood amusements, at least my grandfather didn't think so. My father was a scholar, left me a library of books. But I learned how to shoot and ride, too. I mostly kept to myself, but there was one boy I spent time with after I went to live at my grandfather's. As we grew, so did our friendship..." His voice tightened, and he struggled to continue. "His father became one of the wealthiest men in town but had a dislike for banks. Said there were too many robberies, so he kept his money hidden in a safe."

His laugh came dry at the dark irony of it. Disgusted with himself, he realized he was dancing around the subject. He never knew how difficult it would be to come right out and say the words and to know just what words to say.

"The night the fire broke out, I...had a sense things weren't right. By the time I got to my friend's house, the place was in flames. I heard him cry out from inside and ran in to try to save him. I didn't make it in time. Later, I was told, both he and his father burned in the fire."

He refrained from speaking of his own entrapment and injuries, of how Chester was returning from town and saw him run inside and recognized he was in trouble. He neglected to tell her how the man then pulled him out of the burning house and took him to his mother, who saved his life but could do nothing for the ruin of his face. They were the worst of his scars, worse than the reddened patches on his shoulder and back.

He could never speak of his disfigurement to anyone. Let her think he wore the mask to hide his identity and for no other reason. He couldn't bear to witness her fear or disgust.

Christopher pulled in a shaky breath, forcing himself to relay the rest.

"Someone swore they'd seen me set fire to the house. Said I took the money and murdered both men. My friend. His father. Two bodies were found in the rubble, one still in his bed…"

At the sound of her quiet gasp, he bowed his head, sure she, like the others, now condemned him. Her gentle fingers on his sleeve startled him into looking her way.

"Surely, once you explained what happened, you were able to clear your name?" she asked.

"You would think it would be that easy," he said, a wry twist to his sad words. "But no. As a boy, I'd done my fair share of fibbing, and when I slipped into my grandfather's house weeks later after dark to explain, he accused me of slipping back to my old ways. He was a stern man, and since I didn't show my face straightaway, the evidence built up against me. A second witness told the sheriff that they'd overheard me suggest the scheme to my friend—to rob his father and take off for parts unknown. That was a lie. I never said any such thing."

But *someone* had. And because of that and the act of

framing Christopher, he had suspected the identity of the culprit who spread the fuel of deceit—and the flames. He had not been wrong. In secret, he had hunted down his enemy and trailed him to this area.

"My grandfather ordered me to get out, said I was dead to him. That same night, I visited the girl I thought I would marry. I hid in the trees and waited for her to come outside. She screamed when she saw me and threatened to turn me in…"

The words came forced through gritted teeth. Carla had screamed, not because of his alleged crimes, but because she'd seen beneath his mask. In wanting to believe she could still accept and love him, he had shown her the damage when she first exhibited relief to see him. But she had been repulsed and backed away as if he should be under quarantine, and he had quickly replaced the mask. Christopher sometimes wondered if he had come out unscathed, if Carla would have been more sympathetic and inclined to help him when he'd asked for food and to hide in her barn for one night, rather than order Christopher away and threaten to call her father to bring his shotgun if he didn't go.

He shook his head. "Things only got worse. I hid from the law and everyone else while trying to find my accuser. My search brought me here. But before I left Oregon, I learned my grandfather's heart gave out. I suppose the scandal became too much for him. I had hoped that I could get him to see the truth, catch the real criminal and bring him to justice. So my grandfather would know I hadn't really turned into the black devil he called me. But it's too late for that." He shook his head sadly. "It's too late for a lot of things."

"It's not too late for everything."

Throughout his retelling, she kept her hand in place

above his wrist, and now he felt the gentle squeeze of her fingers.

Stunned to hear that her voice contained the same sweet softness as before, when he had expected it to be full of reproach or disdain, he looked at her. "What do you mean?"

"Your life isn't over, Christopher. You've lost so much, and I can't imagine what that must have been like for you. But there's plenty of room to rebuild and start afresh. From ashes to joy."

He shook his head in confusion. "I don't understand."

" 'To give unto them beauty for ashes, the oil of joy for mourning, the garment of praise for the spirit of heaviness…' " In the darkness, he made out the gentle curve of her lips lifting in a smile. "It's one of my favorite verses. So full of hope."

He nodded softly but said nothing, shaken by how readily she accepted him after hearing his dark tale, how she *believed* him when no one else had. Erica was so different from the rest of the women he'd known. A world of difference compared to Carla, whom he hadn't really known at all. His heart felt overwhelmed to the point of bursting, both by at last speaking the awful words and by the gift of this woman who believed in his reputation. She proved it with every day he knew her; she proved it now. He blinked away the stinging moisture that had settled in his eyes.

"Christopher…" Her voice came even softer, little above a whisper. "Tell me how I can help you."

"You've already done it, more than you know."

His hand lifted to touch her cheek, his fingertips daring a caress against her skin. It had the texture of velvet, like the petal of a rose. Before he could question his sanity, he leaned in, pressing his lips lightly to hers.

He felt the faint and surprised inhalation of her breath,

but she didn't pull back. Tenderly, his lips moved over hers, learning their delicate contours.

Her hands lifted flat against his chest, but she didn't push him away. And at their quiet upward slide, he was lost in her sweetness.

He stole the chill from her lips, warming them with his breath. Cradling her face between his hands, he increased the pressure on her mouth that was so giving, so soft and gentle and trusting, until lost in pleasure he hadn't known in well over a year, he deepened the kiss far beyond what he intended.

Her eager little moan and the clutch of her hands grabbing his shirt brought him to sudden awareness. Quickly he pulled away, blinking fast to bring his rattled senses together, then dropped his hands from her face.

Pushing himself hurriedly to his feet, he turned his back to her. "That shouldn't have happened." His voice came hoarse.

A brief silence, then the rustle of her skirts grew close. "It's all right. I–I'm not upset."

Her words came breathless, wondering and awed, and he shook his head, not daring to look at her. His chaotic feelings still teetered on the brink of all they had shared, and he feared that if he took one more glimpse of her sweet face, he would repeat what just happened.

"You have to forget about me. This is wrong. We can't see each other again. For your own safety, you have to forget about me and…stay away." His voice lowered a pitch. "I mean it, Erica. Don't try to find me again."

Before she could protest, he hurried toward his horse and untied it.

"Christopher… ?"

He ignored the hurt confusion in her voice, telling himself it was for her own good that he did this, and without a backward glance rode off into the darkness.

Chapter 8

Throughout that night and the next two days, Erica felt as if she walked in a fog of shock and uncertainty. She would not soon forget Christopher's story. Or his kiss. Unlike the first time he kissed her, no more than a gentle press of his lips to hers, their second kiss had been filled with passion, instilling her with a warm breathlessness and urgency she felt helpless to comprehend or explain. She had not wished him to end it and felt stunned by her surprising lack of self-discipline.

With no mother to talk to about such things—certainly she couldn't speak to her father, even if he did know of Christopher's existence!—she felt adrift in the river of her muddled thoughts and without an oar to paddle. Nora was the closest thing to a mother she had, and though Erica had apologized to her for getting so upset after learning the truth of her heritage, Nora had given Erica plenty of distance since then.

Unable to get Christopher out of her thoughts—not that she wished to, and she certainly had no intention of letting their last meeting be a final good-bye—she laid down her unread book, left the parlor, and walked into the kitchen.

"Hello, Nora," she said cheerily.

Nora gave a stiff nod. "Miss Erica."

Erica withheld a sigh. Whenever matters became tense between them, Nora added the formal address to her name. Most likely a matter of hurt pride, since Nora was considered family and knew that.

"I need some advice." Erica grabbed a dish towel without being told and moved to stand beside Nora, who washed dishes. She took the wet plate from Nora's hand. "Will you help me?"

Nora glanced at her warily. "If I can."

With the subject open before her, Erica now felt uneasy about how to proceed. She suddenly realized she didn't wish to share that special moment between her and Christopher with anyone. An idea illuminated her mind.

"In one of the novels I read recently, a lady receives a kiss from a gentleman. It makes her feel warm and…faint." Erica felt a similar warmth flush her face when Nora directed a sharp glance her way. "Was the kiss wrong for the lady to allow, especially since she didn't know the gentleman for long?"

"How long?"

"Weeks."

Nora very slowly washed the next plate. "A simple kiss is not wrong. If the man is special to the woman, a husband or a beau. Holding hands, a hug…that is acceptable. But a kiss can also be dangerous."

"Dangerous?"

Nora's face flushed deep red. Erica felt like a naive child instead of a knowledgeable woman of twenty. But she'd had no one to explain such things to her and, until Christopher's kisses, had not given a great deal of thought to such matters.

"Those feelings can lead to foolish decisions that can be harmful if a covenant of marriage is not involved. That is where it is wise to practice self-control, as the Good Book teaches." Now the dishrag jerked quickly with her movements as Nora hurried through one dish and grabbed another without stopping. Erica barely got the second one dry and put away on the shelf before Nora finished the next. "You never want to find yourself in such a situation. It is best to use common sense and avoid it, even if at the time you feel it's what you desire."

Erica dazedly nodded, befuddled with the mysterious nuances of the conversation. But she understood enough to realize that Nora spoke directly to her, as if knowing the discussion had little to do with a character from a novel.

"Did Christopher kiss you, Erica?" Nora asked at last.

Relieved that she had dispensed with the formality, but ill at ease to have the subject pinned on her, Erica only managed another slight nod.

Nora's brows drew together in concern. "Be careful, my dear. I do not wish to see you hurt."

"Christopher wouldn't hurt me. He's not like that," she defended, though his abrupt departure after initiating such closeness had hurt her a great deal. "He left directly afterward."

Nora gave a tight nod. "That is good. Putting distance between you is good."

"But why?"

She hesitated then again looked at Erica. "I will tell you more, when it's acceptable to do so."

Acceptable? "And when will that be?" Erica refrained

from ending on an impatient note, not wishing to sound like a fretful child.

"When you are to wed, the night before you go to live with your bridegroom. We will speak more of these things, as my mama did for me."

Erica wished to know more now. She was no longer a child, but their conversation had been awkward at best. Time to grow accustomed to the idea might benefit them both and ease that moment. Though at Nora's mention of a wedding, Erica wondered if that day would ever arrive for her. She barely knew Christopher, but already he secured a strong place in her heart that felt as if it could become permanent. He had been brave to run into a burning building to try to save his friend, and she felt angry at the beast who framed him for such a reprehensible crime. That thought spawned another. It was amazing that Christopher had escaped without injury…

"You are thinking of him now, yes?" Nora prodded gently.

Erica turned to place the dried forks into the little wooden box for the cutlery. She closed the lid and placed it back, high on the shelf.

"I only wish I could understand him," she fretted. Had he not realized that she wished to be his ally? Why had he suddenly felt the urgent need to flee and warn her away from ever seeing him again? His actions before that had proven he wanted her near…

"Erica, has Christopher not behaved like a gentleman with you?"

Jarred from her troubling memories, she felt another flush and quickly spoke: "Oh, no. He's been very courteous since I've come to know him."

"That is good." Nora's tone came softer and reassured. Erica had no wish to continue the awkward conversation and asked a second question that burned in her mind since the revelation about her heritage: "You knew my mother as well as my father did, I expect. I wish to know more about her. Will you tell me what you know?"

Nora laughed, also clearly relieved to change the topic. "There isn't much I haven't told you already."

"No, not that mother. The woman who gave birth to me. Since you were together on the same wagon train I assume you knew her, too?"

Nora's expression grew serious. "Ah, of course you would wish to know about Sarah, your mother…. My husband had died. I was accompanying my aunt and uncle to the northwest, along with my cousin…"

Erica nodded, remembering what she knew about Nora's family. Their second winter in Washington, the three had perished from an accident when their wagon lost a wheel and fell down an embankment. At the Chandlers' invitation, Nora had come to work for and live with Erica's family.

"Despite being with family," Nora continued, "I was lonely. My cousin was ten and kept to herself, keeping company with her doll. She did not like me, but she did not like anyone. She never wanted to leave Pennsylvania." Nora shrugged. "My aunt and uncle barely said a word to me or to each other. They did not socialize well with people. Your mother was lonely, too." She laughed as if at a fond memory. "We were very different, Sarah and I. She was beautiful, an opera singer, and I was a plain, simple farm widow, a young girl who had married a man fifteen years older. In the East, our paths never would have crossed, but on the trail, everyone was the same and needed to rely on one another to survive. Once your mother grew big with child, she could not do so much, and I helped. We became good friends." Nora washed the last plate and handed it to Erica. "Put that away, and I will put more coffee on. Then we will sit at the table and I will tell you all you wish to know about your mama."

Erica nodded, entranced with the idea, having had no concept that Nora knew her mother so well.

Moments later, Nora continued. "Your mother, she loved you very much. She was so happy when you were born. I was there. She named you for your grandmother. You were such a pretty thing and still are. So much like Sarah in many ways." She sighed, her smile sad. "Early, when the journey was still new, in the evenings she would sing for your father. Her voice carried through the camp and brought joy to many who heard it."

"What happened to her?" Erica asked softly.

Nora's features sobered. "It was very hard on the trail. Too hard for a woman who had newly given birth and was not accustomed to such a life. Your father, Roland Waverly, had been her manager at the opera house, and all she knew how to do was sing. She could barely cook and knew little of chores. With my help, she tried hard to succeed, and your father, he loved her very much, no matter if she failed. She loved him the same and told me she owed him everything. He had saved her from a dangerous admirer who became…forceful with his attentions one night after the opera. It was after that they fell in love."

Erica gaped at Nora. From what she had heard about the man who sired her, she hadn't thought him capable of love for anyone, or that he had a heart at all. And in that instant, in her mind they were no longer unknown ghosts of a newly discovered past. Now they had names—Roland and Sarah—a couple who had shared hopes and fears and dreams. She was a part of them. They had become more familiar to her, no longer nameless strangers, and Erica felt shaken by the intensity of feeling that gripped her heart and brought a film of tears to her eyes. She swiped them away with her napkin, on the pretext of first wiping her mouth.

"Why did he go to California?" She didn't ask why he didn't take her with him. Even if Nora knew, Erica wasn't sure she wanted to hear it.

"That was their original destination. Your mother was to sing there."

"My mother didn't like singing in the East?"

"I never understood why they left. They were both uneasy with speaking of their life before. I assumed something had happened to force their decision to go. That your father was in trouble. He was a cold man to others, but losing your mother—it devastated him. He was beside himself with grief and swore to get vengeance on the wagon master for not heeding his wishes."

This was the first Erica had heard of such a thing. "Papa didn't tell me that."

"It's not a pretty story. Not one you might wish to hear."

Erica felt a jolt at the echo of Christopher's words.

"But I do want to hear it. I want to hear all of it."

Nora nodded. "Very well. I will tell you." She sipped her coffee then set it down, growing thoughtful. "Sarah was weak most of the time, but she grew truly ill, with fever. She feared you would become ill and stopped giving you her milk. You were not yet two months. Another woman in our party had a child and offered to nurse you, too. Despite her fears, your mother grew panicked when you left her sight and wanted you with her often, concerned something might happen to you. Your father grew frantic and asked the wagon master for a day to camp, telling him Sarah could not possibly travel over such rough land in her condition and needed rest. The wagon master, Mr. Williams, said he had to think of the entire party's welfare and the need to cross the mountains before winter. He told your father he could not risk so many lives to save one woman. But Sarah was all that mattered to your father. And the wagon master's words enraged him. The journey proved too much for poor Sarah. A few nights later, she died while holding you in her arms." Nora's voice grew sad with the memory. "Your father took a gun and went after the wagon master. Some men stopped him before he could pull the trigger, but he swore he would hunt Mr. Williams down unto his dying day and make him pay for what he'd done to Sarah, that life did not matter without her."

Erica shook her head, stunned and not knowing what to say or ask next.

"The morning after the day they buried Sarah, your father disappeared without telling anyone. He left while everyone was sleeping. He was never heard from again."

Erica blinked in surprise. "Then you don't know if he even made it to California?"

"No. No one does."

Erica pondered this new revelation.

"He did not dislike you, as you must think." Nora's voice was very soft. "But he was mad with grief. I think he feared to care for someone so small, in the wilderness, with no idea how to do so... . You can have no idea what it was like, with no civilization and very few rivers or even trees to give shade, week after week. Just prairie grass and dirt and wind. And there were other dangers, like the threats of many natives who first lived on the land. He knew that you would be looked after, if that is any consolation."

It was and it wasn't.

"Nora, if you and my mother were so close, why didn't she ask you to take me? Or the woman who nursed me, why didn't she take me?"

"I did consider it; you had become very special to me. But a child needs two parents, and I was alone, newly widowed, and dependent on my uncle's charity. The other woman had five girls and no boys, and her husband refused to take another."

"So the Chandlers offered to take me?"

"Yes. Your mother would have been pleased. She liked them very much. They had been married ten years and were childless. They stepped forward and took you to their wagon. No one stopped them. Many were relieved, having feared what would become of you. I was happy, knowing you would be well cared for. I had seen their kindness, often helping out a neighbor. When I was alone and they came forward, asking if I would like to work for them, I considered it a gift from God. To work for such a couple and be in the same house with Sarah's child, watching you grow up…" Tears glistened in her eyes. "It was more than I could have hoped for. At times, I have felt like your mother as well."

"After Mama died, I thought of you as one," Erica admitted and laid her hand over Nora's, squeezing it. "I was very upset to learn I was adopted and that it was kept a secret from me for so long, but now I feel fortunate to learn I had three mothers who loved me."

Nora laughed and nodded.

Erica's father suddenly walked through the door. "Do I smell fresh coffee?"

The women smiled at each other, and Nora hurried to pour him a cup. He thanked her as she set it down before him, where he'd taken a seat next to Nora's.

Erica couldn't help but notice the sudden bloom in Nora's cheeks and her shy, girlish smile. Erica stared. Mercy, did Nora have feelings for *her father*? She shouldn't be surprised. They had known each other long, since before Erica was born, but this revelation to top all else was just too much to take in at the moment.

Emotionally drained from what she had learned of her blood parents, much of it contrary to what she supposed, Erica hugged her kind guardians and bade them good night, leaving for her room.

Once there, she stood near the window that looked out onto the part of the forest where she had last been with Christopher. She wondered what had become of him and where he had gone, while reflecting on all she had just learned. The two subjects paralleled, finding common ground, and her eyes grew wide when she remembered Nora's account of her father's grief.

Christopher had also suffered a great tragedy, feeling as if he'd lost everything…

Surely his plan didn't include…?

His story quickly unveiled in her mind—all he had said, all he withheld, evident by his guarded remarks and hesitant answers and the enigmatic manner in which he conducted himself. And suddenly, she knew his true reason for coming to Washington. Knew also that she must find him and talk him out of it before he did something foolish they would both live to regret.

Chapter 9

Christopher rubbed the dry rag along the barrel of his gun, feeling as if he lived in a tempest of confusion.

One minute he followed the accepted course of wisdom, keeping his distance from Erica as he should, as he must.

The next, he followed his foolish heart, wishing for something that could never happen.

Even if he didn't now have a face that could frighten little children into having nightmares for the rest of their young lives and cause them to run screaming the other way, he was still an outlaw in the eyes of the populace. Erica's relationship with her father had become tenuous at best, due to her shock in finding out she wasn't his blood-born daughter, and Christopher wanted no part in straining that bond further by making her choose sides. Which she would have to do if she continued to see him. She couldn't be a loyal daughter and keep Christopher secret at the same time.

So he had told her they couldn't see each other anymore. But not before giving in to the need that burned inside him to kiss her. Her clear acceptance and concern had pushed him over that unstable brink. He had reached out for her in joyful relief to find someone who believed in him—and to have that someone be Erica. More than a year was a long time to go without a hug, a gentle word, any form of affection, and he had carried the kiss far beyond what he should have. It had been a mistake to kiss her at all. And the hurt confusion in her voice when she called out after him once he'd fled from her side only made the guilt sting worse.

He had kissed her as a man would kiss his wife.

He grimaced at his foolishness. No matter his circumstances, any chance to initiate something more with Erica was doomed. If he had come out unscathed from the fire and retained his old face, he would still be on the run because of the bounty on his head. And if he was no longer a hunted man, he would still have this wretched face.

Either way, he could not win. Either way, he must let her go. Because either way, she would come to loathe him.

Christopher paused in his task and closed his eyes. Prudent wisdom might avert more heartache for both of them, but it didn't stop him from missing her. How could she impact his life so strongly when he had known her such a short time?

Often at night, when the world lay peaceful, the crackling fire and the occasional hoot of an owl or distant howl of a wolf the chief sounds heard, inside his mind he would remember her voice, her beautiful songs of comfort and hope. And his soul would long to find that peace again...

"Mama, why are those people crying?"
His mother held his hand as they walked down the

road and past a group of women dressed in black. She nodded to them and waited until they were out of earshot before she answered. "Because they lost someone very dear, and at the moment, they feel as if their lives are over."

He thought about that. "Are they over?"

"Oh no, my son, far from it. But they will learn that, as the days pass and the pain ebbs, God will always be there for them, to give comfort and help them weather the storms."

"Will God always be there for me?"

"Always, my sweet."

He smiled then grew somber. "Do I have to lose someone first?"

"No, but one day you will. Everyone does."

"But why? I don't want to lose anyone! Mama, you won't leave me, will you?"

She stopped and hunched down to him, her gentle blue eyes at a level with his as she rested her hands on his shoulders. "There is a beginning and an end to everything in this life, Christopher, a cycle no one can break. It's just the way of things. And yes, someday when the time is right I will go to heaven to be with your two little sisters, and you must remember all I have told you today."

"I don't want you to go! I don't want the time to be right."

"There, there." She wiped a tear that trickled from beneath his eyes then drew him close in a brief hug. "Going on to glory is a beautiful thing, dear, don't you fret so. No one knows their appointed time, and that's why we must make the most of each moment we have. No matter what happens, I'll always be here." She rested her hand over his heart. "And

you'll never lose God. He's always there, too, unless you *are the one to walk away from Him. Even then, He'll always be patiently waiting for you to come back, as long as you walk the face of the earth."*

"I would never walk away from God. I don't want to go to that place Preacher Davies talks about of fire and prim-stone."

She chuckled. "No, fire and brimstone is not for my little boy. Now, enough of these tears, let's go find Papa and have that picnic!"

Christopher sat very still as the bittersweet memory of that summer day with his mother flashed through his mind with the suddenness of a brisk wind. She could not have known that her appointed time would come that winter, hers and Papa's both, and Christopher would be left an orphan at the age of five, in the care of her crotchety father who barely tolerated children.

Somberly, he continued cleaning his gun. His mother would not approve of the course he'd chosen, but Christopher saw that he had little choice. He had done all he said he would never do.

And his life felt as if it had come to a close.

A crackle in the underbrush alerted him to company. With his gun in pieces, he whipped around and grabbed his rifle, aiming it in that direction. The noise grew louder, the bushes stirred, and he cocked the hammer.

"Come out of hiding and make yourself known," he commanded in a low, stern voice. "Or I'll shoot and ask questions later."

"It's only me! Don't shoot!"

Christopher groaned and lowered his rifle, condemning the sudden eager lurch of his heart to hear her sweet voice again. The bushes parted, and into his camp stepped the woman he had dreamed about almost every night since meeting her.

"What do you want?" he growled without welcome, hoping to scare her away or get her so upset she would go on her own initiative.

He should have known better. He also should have known that no matter where he might have relocated, she would have found him, as stubborn as she was. He needn't have bothered to move his camp to another location the second time.

"Don't you be cross with me." Erica's words came just as petulant. "If anything, *I* deserve that right, with the way you just left me standing there three nights ago."

He nodded, curtly tossing the rifle down. "Yes, you do. So why hunt me out again? To tell me that? To yell at me?"

Her manner instantly changed, her features going soft and putting him on his guard.

"I don't want to yell at you, Christopher. I don't want to fight with you at all."

He looked back down to his dismantled gun and resumed his cleaning.

"I told you to stay away."

"Yes, but why?"

Disbelief that she would ask brought his eyes snapping back to hers. "I told you *why*. Have you forgotten so quickly that I'm wanted by the law—by *your father*?"

She winced at his emphasis. "Yes, I know. But what has changed that is different than before? The state of those affairs was the same when I first met you, but you came to my house at my invitation…"

"You didn't know who I was then."

"And now I do. I had hoped that you would have seen that doesn't change the way I feel about—that, that I believe you when you say you're innocent."

Her last words tumbled over themselves, awkward, and he blew out an exasperated breath, his strokes with the rag coming more forceful.

"What do you want, Erica?"

She didn't answer straightaway.

"Is that for him?"

At her grim words, he looked up. "What are you talking about?"

"The gun." Her focus remained on his hands. "Do you plan to use that on him?"

His hands clenched around the barrel then relaxed. "You don't know what you're talking about."

"I hope that's true," she said sincerely, "but I don't think it is."

"You should go home," he said quietly.

"Is that your answer to everything, Christopher? To send me home or run off yourself when the questions become too uncomfortable? To push me—and everyone else—away?"

"Who else would I push away?" he gritted out and set the barrel down. "There is no one else."

"Which is why you need me to help you."

In disgust, he rose to his feet and threw down the rag. He considered walking off, but she would only follow.

"And what exactly do you think you can do to help me? Take the bounty off my head? Bring my grandfather back from the grave? Or maybe you can chase back the sun and the moon to the night of the fire and prevent it from ever happening!"

"I can do my best to talk you out of what you have planned and hope to get you to see it's a huge mistake," she answered softly, unaffected by his sarcasm. "One that could destroy you."

He furrowed his brow and turned away. "And what makes you think that hasn't happened already?"

"You're alive. You're standing here, in front of me, healthy and whole. You have an opportunity to change your future."

He laughed with a snort of disdain. Healthy, maybe— but whole? How little she knew!

"And how do you propose I do that?" he answered her last statement.

"By refusing to become the type of man you're now hunting. And I use the word in the literal sense."

He grew very still.

"You have no plans to find the man who framed you and bring him to legal justice to be tried in a court of law. You want to find him so you can *execute revenge*. You mean to *kill* him."

Stunned that she had discovered his true intent, he said nothing for a moment. "How did you figure it out?" The words escaped of their own initiative. After he breathed them into the air, he wished he could snatch them back.

She inhaled a sharp gasp and let her breath out slowly. "I had hoped I was jumping to all the wrong conclusions, but I had to hear it from you…. I remembered things you said, both the other night and in the past. And the look in your eyes when you said them. It came to me because of something Nora told me, about my birth father, about his need to seek vengeance and why."

His eyes fell shut.

"And now that you know?"

"Christopher…"

He heard the rustle of her steps as she moved to stand before him and put a hand to his shoulder. "You can't do this. You aren't like this."

"The truth is, Erica, you don't know what I'm like."

"I know enough to realize that you're a man who was raised with a strong code of ethics. You not only helped me out, more than once, you tried to save the life of your friend."

Angered by her words, he wrenched away from her hold, again looking in another direction. "No—you don't know me."

"Are you saying what you told me the other night was a lie?"

"I didn't say that."

"Then it was true?"

"Yes, it was true," he said between clenched teeth.

"Then I stand by what I say. Any man who would put others first, at risk to his own safety, his own *life*, is not the sort who can kill an unarmed man in cold blood."

He blew out a harsh breath, squeezing his eyes shut. "Just—stay out of it, Erica. I told you to stay away from all this, from me. You should have listened."

"I couldn't, because I happen to care."

At the sudden memory of seeing *them* together, a grim thought entered his mind. "Or maybe you're hoping to protect him. Is that why you're really here, Erica? To talk me out of giving that scoundrel what he deserves?"

"Those aren't exactly the words I would use—"

"Then you admit it?" he snarled, grabbing her shoulders.

"Admit that I don't want to see you take a human life? Yes! Of course I admit that. If you kill him, you will have sealed your own fate!"

"How long have you been working for him? Have you told him where I am?"

"What?" She shook her head in confusion. "I have no idea what you're talking about. How would I know this man? I don't even know who he is!" Her eyes sparkled with sudden awareness. "But *you* do. Of course you do! You followed him here, to Barretts Grove. He's living in town, isn't he? Who is he, Christopher?"

Instantly, he went on his guard. If she really didn't know his enemy's identity, he had no intention of getting her more involved and putting her in harm's way. But if this was all an act to win Christopher's trust and persuade him to tell her what he knew, she might tip off his enemy, who could then flee from justice again.

She had pieced together Christopher's true intent; she was clever, though it pained him to believe anything malicious about her nature. She didn't owe him her loyalty, but he couldn't give her his trust.

"You won't tell me because you don't believe me," she whispered, hurt.

He released his hold on her shoulders and moved away, his gaze dropping to his gun lying in pieces on the ground…when whole, a significant tool. As it now was, broken apart, worthless. So much like the story of his life.

"I have learned to put my faith in no one. It's what has kept me alive."

Another lapse of silence passed.

"Christopher, have you ever killed a man, even if only in self-defense?"

He drew his brows together. "No."

"It never leaves you. It haunts you day and night, that memory of ending a life."

He turned to look at her. "And how would you know that?"

"One day, when I visited my father at the jailhouse, I heard one of the prisoners locked up there confessing a crime. It ate away at him. He couldn't sleep at night because he was haunted by nightmares of what he'd done."

He shook his head in impatience and looked toward the wall of trees again.

"Christopher, I would never betray you. I would never seek to do you harm. I never want to hurt you."

He sighed wearily. "I really wish I could believe that. You have no idea how much."

She blinked away the tears stinging her eyes. "I suppose then, until you can, I'll have to do whatever I can to gain your trust."

To Erica, his good faith in her would be more precious than any reward he thought she might be after.

After hearing his tragic story, she wasn't angry with his inability to place faith in her; if the roles were reversed, she would also have a difficult time trusting. But that didn't take away the sting of his reaction. How could he think that she would be so spiteful as to side with his enemy, the man who deserved to be behind bars? Did Christopher not realize how she felt about him, that she would do anything for him because she cared so strongly for him?

The deep affection had been there for some time, lying below the surface of her thoughts and resting deep within the core of her heart. In her confusion with all else, she had kept it safely hidden, but now she let the truth gently seep into her mind, warm and reassuring, making her more determined than ever to make him see reason.

If he went through with his plan, she would lose so much, too.

She would lose him.

Because of the rigid set of his shoulders and the distrust in his eyes, wounding her to the quick, she withheld her feelings. It would be mortifying if she spoke and he didn't feel the same. Yet if she did speak, and he cared for her, too, maybe that could be the impetus to force him to give up such a dreadful scheme.

As she watched, a void filled his eyes, as if the mask now covered more than his face. The distant, impersonal manner in which he looked at her killed such hope, but she wouldn't give up.

"Will you at least agree to speak to my father, in a non-hostile environment?"

The detachment left to be replaced by incredulity. He looked at her as if she were mad.

"You must be joking."

"No. Trust me, I feel little like laughing at the moment."

"You want me to have a heart-to-heart with the sheriff?" he asked wryly. "Why not just lead me by a rope and lock me in a cell!"

"Because I believe you," she responded with quiet conviction. "Which is another reason I haven't told my father about this…"

At her frank admission, he lowered his eyes as if moved and ashamed.

"I want you to be the one to do that."

His eyes snapped to hers. "Your father is the *sheriff*, Erica. He will feel duty bound to throw me in jail because of the warrant, no questions asked."

"My father is a fair man. He clearly knows how to keep a secret if needed, and I can promise you this: he'll listen with an open mind. He doesn't tote his guns and wear a badge out of some overrated sense of pride in his title. He truly cares about people. He cares about justice. And you were horribly wronged."

He shook his head slightly, distant again as he looked at the ground. Clearly he wasn't persuaded.

"I know you don't trust me," she whispered, "but it should say something on my behalf that I've kept silent this long. For you. It's been difficult, but I said nothing. I never even told my father we met." She hesitated then moved forward, touching his arm. "Let me speak with him, to see if he would be agreeable to a peaceful meeting. He has never liked to see the innocent made to suffer. Proof of that is how he took another man's child, left in the wilderness, and made her his own."

Christopher remained silent a long time but didn't move away, and she didn't drop her hand from his sleeve.

"The place where we met," he said at last without looking at her, "at the bottom of the hill. Bring him there tomorrow. After noon. No one else. Not that deputy. Just your father."

Her heart jolted with excitement that he had agreed, albeit tensely, and the warmth of relief filled her.

"I have a good feeling about this, Christopher. You won't regret it."

He gave no reply, and she dropped her hand from his arm.

"I should go. Nora will be wondering where I am."

He offered a brief nod.

"All right. Well, good-bye." She turned back to the area from which she'd come. Night would be falling soon, and his new campsite was deeper in the forest. She had almost given up twice before she found him, but he hadn't really worked to cover his trail, and she had been determined. Now she didn't want to risk getting lost and having to find her way out of the trees in the pitch dark.

"Erica, I've never told anyone all of what I told you."

Her heart skipped a beat at his quiet confession that seemed somehow torn from him. By the time she turned around and looked back into the clearing, Christopher had disappeared.

Her smile came shaky, and she felt a rush of grateful

tears. In his farewell she understood what he'd really been saying, that with what small amount of trust he was able to give, he had given it only to her.

And she would not fail him.

Chapter 10

Christopher rode a lengthy distance behind Erica, far enough that she wouldn't hear him behind her, close enough to keep her in his sights and see to her safety. Once he saw the frame house and watched her disappear into the stable, he turned his horse around.

Had he been a fool to agree to her appeal? Her persuasive words coming so soon after the memory of that summer day with his mother had put an unexpected crack in his resolve to play hunter and executioner, one wide enough to question his morbid goal. What he once strongly desired, the sole reason for his existence, had shifted in magnitude, other things now holding more value. And Erica was at the core of it all, muddying his objective. As foolish as it was impossible, as much as he didn't want her there, she had moved into his life with her willful drive and tender trust. Never one to back down, she had forced him to look forward and to question…

And he was tired of this existence. Tired of jumping at every snap and crackle in the forest, always wondering if his demise loomed near and a mob would find and garrote him. Tired of living in a bedroll with only salmon, beans, and berries and the occasional squirrel or rabbit to fill the ache in his belly. Tired of huddling under oilskin or finding some shelter of nature when the relentless rains poured for three seasons. He wanted to sleep in a real bed and ride in the daylight. He longed to walk among others in town without the constant fear of being recognized. He yearned for acceptance—with the mask or without it. The last was no more than a wishful fantasy. But the rest of what Erica offered beckoned like a slice of heaven to a desperate man long sweltering in an unseen place not unlike the authentic one old Preacher Davies warned about. This place, a painful emptiness within his heart, where Christopher endured continual torment that sometimes burned like hellfire in his soul.

And so, he had decided.

He would stay hidden, in case the sheriff brought anyone other than Erica. He could easily slip into the shadows and become one with the forest again. Hurry back to his camp, saddle his horse, and go.

He didn't worry so much about getting caught; he would evade the law as many times as needed. His real fear stemmed in the worry that Erica would betray him.

Christopher strove hard not to believe that about her and had agreed to the meeting with the hope that she was as trustworthy as she claimed. But after everyone he cared about had hurt him, the prospect was weighty that she would, too, and he tried not to cling too desperately to that hope, instead letting it barely filter into his heart but not giving over to it completely.

The chance to tell his story to a lawman who might

believe it, as Erica seemed to think her father would, as Erica herself had done, proved too tempting a morsel for Christopher. If the sheriff believed him, Christopher could at last stop running. He might not get the grim satisfaction of executing his brand of justice, but justice would be served, and his enemy would be the one swinging from a gibbet for the crimes committed.

A soft breeze brushed against his face, making Christopher wish he could remove the cumbersome mask to feel all of the coolness against his prickling skin, often uncomfortable behind its prison of concealment. But fitting. A strip of hide to cover a beast, rejected and alone.

He stared above the spires of treetops at the patchwork of silver stars on a clear bed of black velvet sky. They seemed to shine brighter than ever before, as if beckoning him to remember.

"As long as you walk the face of the earth..."

Christopher wiped away the sudden tear that leaked from beneath his mask. Suddenly restless, he pushed his horse into a fast gallop, eager for the dark solitude of his camp.

In her excitement, Erica found it hard to sleep. As a result, when she did finally drift off, she ended up waking after dawn and missing her father who'd already left for the jailhouse.

Pushing away her disappointment, she determined to leave quickly and donned a simple dress of sky-blue poplin, befitting her hopeful mood, but Nora stopped her exit, insisting she eat first. Erica could barely force anything down but an apple, managing only to make a dent in the fluffy eggs.

She wondered what Christopher ate this morning, imagining him huddled over his campfire with a tin of beans.

She had spied a small stack there and felt a stroke of guilt to indulge in a hot, full meal, day after day, while he subsisted on next to nothing.

Hopefully this afternoon would put an end to that. She prayed he hadn't changed his mind.

Doubts had plagued her when she first saw the wanted poster. But her belief in his innocence had intensified after last night. And she was eager to get the plan underway to clear his name, so that he could walk among the living again, instead of remaining buried within the tomb he had made for himself in the stillness of the forest.

During her ride home from his campsite, she had experienced a strange sensation, a warm awareness that she wasn't alone. Once she led her mare into the barn, she had turned at the door to see a lone rider turn his horse and head in the other direction. She was convinced that no man guilty of such horrendous crimes would show gallant concern to see to it that a lone woman safely reached her home in the evening. But Christopher had. And she wondered if last night had been the first occasion he so furtively had guarded her.

Nothing about his behavior matched that of a selfish, cold-blooded killer. Each moment she remembered with him further assured her of his innocence. He was unlike the criminals she had glimpsed that her father and the deputy arrested for any number of crimes, some as bad as what Christopher was accused of. Many of those men had been belligerent, cursing and swearing and harsh. Some had claimed their innocence, too, but their violent, dishonorable actions didn't match their words and marked their guilt more likely. She couldn't imagine any of those men seeing a woman safely home in secret. But she could see them as being the source of danger from which a woman would need protection. Protection through men like Christopher.

As she finished her meal, she wondered again who his enemy was. She had talked to many men in her quest for a story, new and familiar faces alike, and she wished now that she had insisted Christopher give her a name. Not that he would have. He always told her only what he wanted her to know at the time, which, except for the tragic tale of his past, was very little. Even in speaking of that, she'd felt as if he still held something back.

She made the trip into town in less time than it usually took, tying Ginger to the post in front of the jailhouse.

"Miss Chandler?"

Erica looked to the source of the voice, at first uncertain, then recognized the stranger who had been with Mr. Millstone.

"Yes, Mister...I'm sorry, we were never introduced."

He took off his hat. "Liam Aldridge."

"I'm in a bit of a hurry, Mr. Aldridge, if this could wait?"

"I'm afraid it cannot."

She looked at him in surprise to hear his answer, noting he seemed even more nervous than the first time she'd seen him. He fidgeted with his hat, twirling the brim.

"I understand you're looking for a story. I have one to tell."

Despite her eagerness to speak to her father, her curiosity was piqued. "Not that I don't appreciate your offer, Mr. Aldridge, but if it's so important, why have you not told your news to one of the current journalists at the paper?"

"It involves someone you know well." He said the words grimly, his manner changed as his dark eyes seemed to impale her with...suspicion? Dislike? Mistrust? In the next instant, the look was gone, and she felt she must have imagined it.

Before she could inquire further, Ralph stepped outside. Upon sight of him, Mr. Aldridge looked away. "I must go." His voice dropped to a confidential whisper. "I— Please, Miss Chandler, if you could meet with me as soon as possible, I would be most grateful."

"Of course, I...suppose..." She barely got the words out before the strange man turned his back on her and walked away.

"Wasn't that the new fellow? What did he want?"

She turned to Ralph and walked toward the stoop. His skeptical blue eyes focused beyond Erica to the departing man.

"Being as there are new faces in Barretts Grove all the time, including yours if we were to consider tenure as those citizens who've been living here at least a year, then yes, I would say he's new to town, and I have no idea what he wanted. Is Father inside?"

Ralph's face went ruddy. "Sorry, Miss Erica. I didn't mean to sound presumptuous. I, well, I don't trust him. Him or his friend. Just be careful."

Erica had learned there were many in town Ralph mistrusted so she didn't give his warning much merit.

"I understand you'll be leaving tomorrow."

He gave a swift nod. "Your father asked me to stay another week, but I can't."

She found that odd since he usually did whatever Father wanted.

"My mother." His face grew a shade darker, and he looked away. "She needs me."

"Of course." She walked up to the door, and he put his hand to the latch to open it then stopped.

"I need to go see to some things, but this is likely good-bye, Erica. I mean, Miss—"

She put a hand to his arm to reassure him. "It's all right. We're friends, and that bond does allow for a certain familiarity. Ralph."

By his answering smile, she had cheered him from his dour mood, and that pleased her. Perhaps she hadn't been fair to him. He had often been overbearing and pretentious, but his heart was noble and there *were* times she had enjoyed his company.

"I wish you the very best always," she added.

He nodded once and opened the door for her.

She swept inside, relieved and nervous to see her father leaning back in his chair and studying a paper. Christopher's wanted poster stared at her from behind him, and she inhaled a gulp of air for courage, breathed a silent prayer for understanding, and strode forward.

"Erica?" Her father straightened and set down his paper.

"Father, I have something I must speak to you about." She directed a glance to the occupied cell, grateful to see the current prisoner, Mr. Flaherty, was asleep on a cot. Likely he was there for being drunk and disorderly and starting another fight at the saloon. She kept her voice low. "This won't wait."

He looked at her and inclined his head. She sank to the chair facing his desk.

With her hands folded in the lap of her skirt, she anxiously rubbed one thumb over the other. "It's about a man who is wanted. There." Her eyes darted behind him then back.

He looked over his shoulder then at her again. "You've seen this man?"

"It's more than that really." She swallowed and looked at her hands. "I know him."

An uneasy silence ensued. Erica quickly broke it.

"While you were in Oregon, I had an accident on the way home, at that hill that faces the river. The one I like to stop at and watch the sunsets from." She cleared her throat, gathering another dose of courage. "A man, that man, helped me back to my horse. He's helped me other times, too." She went into an account of her meetings with Christopher, barely touching the surface but revealing enough to display his good character. "I—I didn't know about that"—she gave a hasty flip of her hand toward the poster— "until a week ago."

Her father regarded her somberly. "And just why haven't you told me this before?"

"Well, I did struggle with what to do. I finally decided that in some cases, the omission of truth isn't exactly a lie."

He glanced down, clearly ill at ease and recalling his own omission.

"I'm sorry. But after hearing Christopher's story, I believe him innocent. I don't think he did any of what they accuse him of. He's just not like that. He wouldn't murder anyone in their beds or set fire to another man's house, or any of it."

He pensively nodded. "While in Oregon, when I got the poster, I talked with a few people who knew this man. They expressed shock that he would do such a thing, said he'd been a quiet boy and didn't seem the type." He studied her. "So tell me, why are you coming to me with this now?"

Uncomfortable, she shifted in her chair. "I haven't felt easy about keeping this from you. And I…I worried that he might seek revenge on the real criminal who did those things." She explained what little she knew of that. "I talked with him last evening, assuring him that you're a fair man, and he's willing to meet with you in a place he's chosen, to tell his story. Anytime after the noon hour, and he asked that you come alone."

He pondered her words, touching his fingertips together and spreading them wide. "I'm surprised you still think me a fair man."

It was the last thing she expected to hear. "Why would you think that?"

"Because I never told you where you came from."

She lowered her eyes to her lap and unclasped her hands, smoothing imaginary wrinkles from her dress. They had never spoken of that night, slipping back into familiar roles but always edged with discomfort and words withheld. "I shouldn't have acted so dreadfully. Crying like I did and running from the room, screaming to be left alone. It was childish."

"It was understandable." He sighed. "I haven't been a good father."

"That's not true—"

"After your mother died," he went on as if she hadn't spoken, "I felt as if my life ended, too. I couldn't stand to be in that house, everywhere I looked I saw her, and I spent more time here. The ache finally eased, but that lifestyle became a habit. I neglected you. I didn't realize you needed me. You seemed happy, always caught up in your music."

Erica's head snapped up, her eyes wide at the revelation. And then it hit her.

"Nora told you."

He nodded curtly. "You should have told me, honey. I never meant to hurt you. It was the last thing I wanted." His voice came more gruff. "There are only two memorable occasions worthy of merit that have happened to me in my fifty-two years. One was the day I married Elizabeth, your mother. The second was the day we took you to our wagon to become part of our family. Our daughter."

Tears burned her eyes, and she left her chair to hurry around the desk and hug him. "I love you, Papa," she breathed, kissing the top of his head and laying her cheek against it, her arms about his neck.

He patted her arm. "You were never more wanted. Don't believe otherwise."

She nodded softly before pulling away. Using her fingertips to wipe the moisture from beneath her eyes, she returned to the matter that brought her here.

"And Christopher?"

He sucked in a deep breath, letting it out heavily. "I admit, I'm torn. Those crimes aren't exactly in the category of stealing a turkey or being drunk and disorderly. Taking a life is serious business, as are all the other charges…"

Her eyes downcast, she nodded. What would she tell Christopher?

"However, after hearing you go on about him so, I can't help but be grateful that he assisted my little girl. He doesn't sound like a villain, and I've had my doubts since my visit through his hometown…." He weighed the facts aloud then gave a short nod. "I'll give him his neutral meeting. I trust your judgment, and if you believe him, I'm inclined to forget my lawful duty for one hour or however long it takes to hear his story."

"Oh, thank you, Papa!" Erica couldn't contain her joy and hugged him again then picked up his timepiece and flipped open the lid. "It's one hour till noon. I'll return then to take you to him." She set the pocket watch back on the desk. "I know you'll feel about him the same way I do."

He peered at her intently, and she felt a flush warm her face.

"And how is that, Erica?" he asked with a new disapproving awareness, as if he could see her hidden feelings for Christopher blazing in her eyes. She feared that they did show and moved to the door.

"Why, that he's innocent of course."

This was partly the reason she'd taken so long to mend differences with her father. Keeping Christopher's secret had made it difficult to be in the same room with him. But the relief she felt to let the truth out and again be at peace with her family left her almost buoyant.

Eager for the hour to fly, Erica decided to use up some of those minutes and made her weekly visit to *The Chronicle*.

The editor grimaced when he saw her enter and stood, grabbing his hat.

"Can't deal with you yet today, too. I have somewhere I need to be." Gruffly he brushed past where she stood just inside the open door.

And a pleasant day to you, too, Mr. Mahoney.

"Miss Chandler, how do," one of the men called out to her. "Any further sightings of the masked ghost bandit?"

She narrowed her eyes at him and left, amid the chortles of the others. If dogged persistence in the face of frequent discouragement was the chief requirement for such work, she would have secured a position long ago. She had hoped to convince the editor that a woman could write just as well as a man, but perhaps the time had come to give up.

At the defeated thought, so contrary to her nature, her heart rebelled, and she headed out the door. She would *never* surrender when it came to her dreams. *All* of them.

"Good day, Miss Chandler." Jake Millstone came up from behind, falling into step beside her.

With the day so perfect, despite the irksome reception just received, she drummed up a smile for him. "It *is* a good day."

He chuckled. "Yes, it is. A lovely one. Seems at last

we've hit the dry season. Might I interest you in a ride through the countryside? My wagon is just over there."

Surprised that he would issue such a request based on the short extent of their acquaintance, which was practically nonexistent, she shook her head. "No, thank you, Mr. Millstone. I have plans later, with my father. Good day."

She walked on. Before she made it to the next building, she again heard him come up behind her. Something hard shoved into her ribs, and she glanced down in shock to see his hand inside his waistcoat, holding something that caused the material to tent toward her. She didn't need to ask to know it was the barrel of a gun.

"Keep walking, nice and easy. You should rethink my invitation." His words were calm, as if they discussed the rise in prices at the general store they approached. "One word, so much as a glance in the wrong direction, and a bullet makes a nasty hole in that pretty fair skin of yours. Now we wouldn't want that, would we? Just smile and nod at me if you understand."

Her heart racing in terror, Erica did as ordered.

"Good. I'm glad we finally understand each other. Now, here's my wagon. Step up right here—that's right, my dear—and remember, I have a gun on you the whole time."

Once seated, Erica shifted her foot to the wagon's edge, slowly easing her hand to her boot top as he went around the wagon. As he walked around the front, his hand with the gun made a threatening movement inside his pocket, and she stilled her hand's progress and pulled it back to her lap. Her eyes darted around her. The jailhouse was too far away to call out for help then duck from the wagon. Two elderly women spoke nearby, and a boy rolled a hoop with a stick on the dusty street. No one in the vicinity looked capable of helping her. Her heart beating fast, Erica remained perfectly still, not wishing anyone to get hurt by a stray bullet.

Her abductor took his position on the wagon seat, untying the reins but never moving the aim of his gun from her. He drove them a short piece from town then shifted her way, no longer concealing his weapon. The sun gleamed down on the silver barrel of the revolver pointed in her direction.

"Before we go farther, give it to me."

"What?" she whispered.

"Whatever you're hiding in your boot. Come now," he said a little more testily when she hesitated. "If you don't, I'll just have to hunt for the treasure myself."

Frowning, she withdrew her small Derringer. He held out his hand for it, and she slapped it in his palm.

"Careful. Nice girls shouldn't play with guns, didn't your daddy ever tell you that?" His eyes brightened in mockery as if he just remembered: "Oh, that's right. Your daddy's the sheriff! Do sheriffs allow their daughters to play with guns? Or are you being naughty?" He pocketed her weapon.

She clenched her teeth at his condescension and her fear. "What is it you want from me?"

He reached out to run a curled finger down her cheek. She tensed and jerked away from his touch, determined to fight him tooth and nail before she would let him near her.

"Ah, my dear Miss Chandler, I've heard about your masked stranger. It's been quite the talk among a number of your townsmen. I heard a few of them ribbing you about it just moments ago. Of course, those at the paper don't believe he exists except in your imagination, which works to my advantage. But we both know differently, don't we?"

She stared in horror at the revelation of Christopher's

enemy, her answer tight in her closed throat and refusing to come.

Jake's handsome face twisted into a snarl. "Now, you're going to take me to him."

Chapter 11

From the moment Christopher woke that morning, he sensed a change in the air. He couldn't place his finger on the difference, assuming it had to do with his nervous anticipation of the upcoming meeting, but it felt like more than that. More extreme than the static in the air, like the atmosphere before an oncoming storm, he felt an expectancy in his soul. Feelings he had long trapped beneath a thick surface of fear and dread and resentment were fighting like new seedlings attempting to break free of the weight that pushed them under.

He knew better than to hope! That only brought heartache when his expectations didn't come to pass. But he couldn't shake this lightness of heart that brought him to prowl the edge of the trees long before the appointed time, though he called himself a fool for daring to believe.

The sound of distant horses halted his impatient movements. The sun's placement in the sky told him the noon hour had not yet approached, and warily he edged closer, hidden behind a tree.

The clearing remained empty. He wondered if he imagined the sound, or perhaps it had been a passing rider. Before he could turn away to resume pacing, Erica's form came into view. The identity of the man with her made his heart crash from the spire of hope where it had so foolishly climbed. His teeth clenched, and he inhaled an angry rush of air.

So, she *had* betrayed him, wishing to trap him. She had brought his *enemy* here, and not a possible friend.

Tears of anguish at her duplicity stung his eyes. His first instinct was to race back to camp and flee the area, again to blend into shadows, but he hesitated.

Something wasn't right.

Jake held her upper arm, walking close by her side with his usual arrogant cockiness, but Erica's movements were tense and erratic, forced, unlike her usual grace. They came to a sudden stop in the clearing.

Christopher gasped in horror as the sunlight flashed on Jake's gun pointed at her side.

Erica tried to control her rapid breathing, but she couldn't contain her dread. His bruising hold on her arm curtailed movement. The gun pressed at her waist banned it.

Nausea rolled in her stomach. She had refused at first, even tried to lead him off course, but he became more terrifying and violent, and she in her fear, wretched coward that she was, had given in and led this fiend to Christopher! From what their tormenter had just told her, he meant to kill him. A silent litany of entreaties went up to her Savior, but on the outside Erica remained still and mute, loath to utter a word and further incite her captor or help him more than she'd been forced. He no longer seemed to care what she did or didn't do, his eyes scanning the trees.

"I know you're there," he called, and Erica winced as he brought the gun from behind and pressed the end of the barrel to her temple. "If you want your lady friend to take her next breath, I strongly advise you to come out from hiding and let me see your face!"

Even as Erica furiously prayed that Christopher would ignore the threat and stay concealed, she heard the rustle of undergrowth.

Her heart plummeted in dismay at the same time she experienced a warm rush of joy to see him, as she always did when he suddenly appeared.

He stepped forward, his stride easy, deceptively relaxed, bearing that quality of latent danger she had come to associate with him. His masked face was a welcome sight, even as she wished he would forget her and escape back into the forest and to safety. He was strong and courageous but no match for a gun. His solemn gaze went to her face, resting there. His jaw went hard as stone when he saw the bruise on her cheek. With her eyes, she begged his forgiveness.

She had become the trap to the only man she had ever strongly cared about, and she could not bear to see his capture.

"Christopher, no—go back! Please, go back!"

She felt their enemy tense behind her.

"So, it really is you," he greeted, a hint of disbelief softening his grim words.

"Let her go." Christopher did not cease his slow, steady advance. "This is between you and me, Jake. She has no part in it."

"I'm not so sure about that." His voice grew eager, like a little boy exulting over his prize. To Erica's horror, he turned the gun away from her and aimed at Christopher, pulling back the hammer. "Of course, once you're out of the way, I can do with Miss Chandler whatever I please. And you can't stop me. You couldn't stop me then, you can't stop me now." A mirthful little laugh bubbled from his throat. "Face it, Christopher, you've lost again. And this time, it's for good. My king has trumped your king. *Checkmate.*"

With their enemy gloating, his attention fully riveted on Christopher, Erica saw her chance and took the risk. She may not be Christopher's queen, but she would do all in her power to protect him.

She slammed her heel down as hard as she could on her attacker's toes at the same time she pushed his arm upward with both hands. The shot went wild, flying into the trees. He yelled a string of curses and painfully stumbled back. She whirled, kneeing him in the groin and reaching for the gun.

The flash of the back of his other hand only just registered before she felt the sharp smack against her unwounded cheek, sending her sprawling to the ground. Before she could scramble up from her prone position, Christopher lunged forward with an inhuman growl. Both men fought, hands at each other's throats. The pistol lay on the ground, close to their feet.

Erica stared in horror and slowly moved to shaky knees to stand, unable to look away from the fury of swinging fists. She winced and gasped with each painful connection to Christopher's face and body. Both men fought with equal skill, on the edge of desperation and anger. Christopher again tackled his enemy to the ground, but the scoundrel got out from under him, rolling with him until Christopher lay beneath.

Erica watched for an opportunity to dart forward and grab the gun, but each of those two times, one of the men suddenly moved close, almost stumbling over the weapon. Quickly scanning the area for something heavy to use for a blow to the head but seeing nothing, she gaped in horror as their attacker brought down his fist to Christopher's jaw, enough to momentarily stun him. Without warning, Jake grabbed the mask, snapping it from Christopher's face.

"*Nooo!*" Christopher howled like a wild and wounded animal.

Erica inhaled a sharp breath, aghast by the sight of the mottled and scarred flesh. Frozen in place, she could only stare.

Their enemy hissed in revulsion then laughed in triumph, grabbing Christopher's gun from its holster and standing to his feet then retrieving his own weapon.

Christopher rolled away, slapping his hand over the right side of his face, not looking at either of them. Erica's heart clenched in pain at his clear humiliation. She transformed her burning heartache into anger.

"Why did you do that?" she snapped.

The scoundrel laughed, rubbing the blood from his nose with his sleeve. "See what a monster he is? Now that I've opened your eyes to the truth of his deceit, you should thank me."

"*Thank* you?" she repeated in disbelief. "You're despicable."

"He never showed you what was beneath the mask, did he? Look, Christopher, look at the horror on her face to see you for what you truly are." The fiend kicked Christopher in the leg. "Come on. Get up. I have no wish to shoot you while you wallow on the ground, though it would be a fitting demise for the beast you've become. But where's the challenge in that?"

Christopher spit blood from his mouth and sat up, glaring at the man. "I may now look the part, but you live it every day."

He reached for his mask, which lay near him, but the brute stepped on it then kicked it out of reach.

"You don't need that anymore," he jeered. "Your secret's out. Miss Chandler has seen the truth. You can't hide any longer."

Christopher said nothing, only rose slowly to his feet, keeping his hand over his face.

"Christopher… ?" she whispered. The well of emotion flooding inside drowned out further words. Her heart bleeding for his pain, Erica wished he would look at her, just once, but he never directed a glance her way.

"You shouldn't have crossed me," their attacker said, his jovial manner disappearing in a rush of one betrayed. "You should have kept your nose out of it."

"You're the one who came to me and told me your sick plan. I wanted no part of it." The pure venom of hatred dripped from Christopher's words. "*You* started that fire and staged it to look as if I did it. For crying out loud, you killed your own father! What kind of sick monster does that? You faked your death, hiring men to point the blame at me, then slipped away into the night, hoping they would find me and string me up to the nearest tree for *your* crimes! How could I have ever called you *friend*?"

"You always were smart, but not smart enough. So you figured it out. Congratulations. But where has it gotten you? On the lam, hated by society, at the end of my gun— and this time, *I* got the girl. Your face used to win them over, not that it mattered as quiet as you were, but it won Carla. The girl *I liked*. And now I'm the prettier of us two." He laughed in delight. "*That's* what I call justice."

"Your father didn't deserve to die. And I didn't deserve this!" Christopher motioned to his hand covering his face.

"My father was a miser who had no intention of letting me see a dollar of that wealth until I was as old and gray as he was. As I told you then, I had no desire to play the obedient son to his every wretched demand. I wanted to strike out on my own."

"With *his* money," Christopher clipped dryly.

"It would have been mine someday. I just rushed the inevitable along." He grinned. "As for you…" He pointed his gun at Christopher. "It didn't have to be like this. *You* made that choice. I offered you a chance to be wealthy for the rest of your days, to live a life of adventure as partners, tycoons striking it rich in the railroad business, and all you had to do was help me that night while he was sleeping. I would have done the hard part—taken the money, staged it as a robbery, set the fire. I just wanted you as a lookout. But as always, you clung to those insane principles of yours." He laughed cruelly. "Where did they ever get you, Christopher? Look at you! A disfigured, pathetic monster. Now, look at me. More money than most men have gained who are twice my age. The ladies, the hotels, the rich food…. I ask you, who has the better lot?"

Reeling with shock, Erica watched the men and listened to their volley of angry words. The entire revelation of Christopher's enemy made her sick and dizzy. Jake Millstone had been *the friend* Christopher tried to save from the fire? *The same man who* did not *die and framed Christopher for his presumed death?*

Christopher hung his head. "The other body they found in the wreckage of your father's home." His voice came quiet. "Who was it?"

"Some misguided soul who thought he could cheat me at cards then lie his way out of it. Don't remember his name. He was passing through town. We stood at the same height and had the same build. Once I followed him from the saloon and shot him, I saw the opportunity for him to take my place and couldn't pass it up."

As he recounted that night, his demeanor changed, a pleased look coming to his face as he filled them in on the missing parts of the story, as if too delighted with his achievements not to share…or perhaps knowing there was no reason to fear their knowledge of his crimes.

Erica shivered at the wild gleam in his eyes and his erratic behavior. She had never seen anyone behave so peculiar, so bizarre, his moods drastically changing. He truly believed himself justified in all he'd done, congenial at one moment, acting betrayed at the next, and lending to the distinct likelihood that Jake Millstone was not just a criminal but also insane.

At the hands of a madman, she found it a struggle to cling to her faith.

She stared at Christopher, silently begging him to look her way, wishing to connect somehow in what might be their final moment together, wishing to relay all of what she felt in her heart and soak up any strength he could give her…

But he kept his face turned away.

The pain of his bruises and cuts were minimal compared to the feelings of helplessness and rage that tore through Christopher. Beneath that flowed the underlying tide of shame that had long become a part of his blood. Shame that he once befriended this unfeeling monster. Shame that he had roped Erica into his problems and her life was now in danger because of his foolishness. Shame that she had seen the truth of his scars…

He could not bear to look at her, could not witness for himself the revulsion on her flawless, beautiful face to see the beast unmasked. Jake wouldn't need to fire a bullet to kill him. That would happen when Christopher saw the truth written in Erica's eyes.

Jake was a beast to the hidden core of his black soul.

But Christopher's outward appearance would always be monstrous.

"It's *your fault* you're the way you are," Jake went on. "You should have never tried to warn him about me. Don't think I don't know that's why you were there that night. Why else would you come after the fight we had?"

"I had hoped to talk you out of it," Christopher said tersely.

"But you wouldn't have stopped there, oh no. Not the saintly Christopher. You would have felt compelled to tell him when I refused to listen." His smile came through clenched teeth. "I know you too well, so I had to act. I cried for help, knowing you wouldn't be able to refrain from doing the noble thing. I slipped out the back before you charged inside. But the fire didn't do what it was supposed to." He frowned. "It was the stable boy, Chester, wasn't it?" Jake pointed an accusatory finger at Christopher. "He saved you from burning and took you to his witch of a mother."

"She has more good in her heart than you have in your little fingernail."

Jake laughed. "She may have saved your life, but she couldn't save your face!"

Christopher bowed his head, reminded of his humiliation.

"Not that it matters anymore," Jake said thoughtfully. "I don't think I'll shoot you after all…. You. Come here."

Christopher didn't need to look to know he spoke to Erica.

"Leave her alone," he growled.

"Now why would I do that? Miss Chandler and I are

just getting acquainted." Jake grabbed his arm and pushed him toward the trees without letting go. Behind, he heard Erica follow. He wanted to yell out to her to run, but Jake would stop her, likely hurt her worse.

At the base of a tree Jake shoved him to the ground.

"Miss Chandler," he ordered, "take this and tie his hands behind him. Don't do anything foolish. I have my gun trained on you."

Christopher felt her come up beside him and gently touch his arm but could not lower his hand from his face.

"Do as I say," Jake ordered, "unless you want to watch her die."

The repulsion of his scars could not begin to compare to the horror of her death, and Jake knew it. With his hand shaking, Christopher did as ordered and brought his other hand behind him.

"I'm so sorry," Erica whispered close to his ear, tears in her voice.

"No talking," Jake said firmly. "There's no need for getting so close either."

Christopher felt the silkiness of Jake's scarf wrap around his crossed wrists.

"Tie it well, Miss Chandler. Too bad there isn't any rope to tie his feet. That will have to make do."

Christopher felt the force of her first tie and winced as the material dug into his wrists. She made a second loop then a third when Jake demanded it, and brought the edges of material to rest in his palm. At the sudden gentle brush of her fingers against his in parting, a tremor went through him, and his eyes inadvertently flicked to hers.

There was none of the horror he expected to see there, but her eyes were filled with pity and sorrow, which stung what little pride he had left. She quickly cast her gaze down behind him then up again, her eyes holding his, until Jake moved forward and hauled her up by one arm.

"We'll be taking our leave now," he said as if they were still friends and bidding each other farewell.

"You're crazy, Jake. You'll never get away with this. Her father's the sheriff! You don't think he'll come after you?"

"Well, of course, I've taken that into account. I have no intention of returning to town. My fiancée and I will be leaving for parts unknown. Don't bother trying to look for us."

Christopher heard Erica's gasp of horror and growled, snapping his eyes to Jake.

"If you so much as harm another hair on her head, I'll kill you."

"Says the man tied at the foot of a tree," Jake said wryly. "I've heard enough from you for a lifetime." He secured Christopher's mask around his mouth, gagging him.

"Come, darling. Our new life awaits." Jake pulled Erica, resisting, toward him.

"Let go of me," she angrily demanded, her palm pressed to his chest as she tried to wrest herself away.

Jake ignored her and stared at Christopher, who glared at him.

"It is worth more to me to know that you'll suffer the torment each day and night of imagining this beauty that *you* could never have lying in my arms, than it is to be merciful by putting a bullet through your brain. Don't get it into your head to try to get free while my back is turned either. If I glance back and see that you've moved so much as a foot, you'll both regret it." Jake quickly pulled Erica toward the hill.

Enraged, Christopher helplessly watched and struggled against the bond, never having known such terror. To see

Erica taken from him, helpless at the hands of an indifferent killer, made his blood run hot and cold.

The distant sounds of jangling harness and hoofbeats fading away increased Christopher's efforts to free himself.

His fingers numb and burning, he remembered the look she'd given him, the tuck of the ties into his hand, the brush of her hand against his fingers before she pulled away. With his fingers he found the knot and, realizing that she had tied the second and third ties loosely, easily worked them undone. He was thankful that Jake had been careless and hadn't taken the time to check her handiwork. Despite that, the first tie was tight, and it took some time for Christopher to work his wrists to loosen the bond, sawing it against the trunk, scraping skin, but at last he broke free and removed the mask from around his mouth.

Tears of fear and fury wet his eyes and trickled against the sensitive skin of his scars, making them sting. He raced back to camp while tying the soft hide in its proper place around his head. Grabbing his rifle, he mounted, leading his stallion through the forest as fast as he was able through the thicket of close-knit trees.

He may have lost her forever after the cruel unmasking, but that didn't erase his strong feelings for her, and he would do all within his power to save her from such a horrible end. If anything, Christopher realized through this ordeal just how much he did love Erica Chandler.

Chapter 12

With Christopher no longer in danger, Erica relaxed as much as possible under the circumstances. Jake Millstone no longer trained his gun on her, now using both hands to hold the reins, but she would be foolish to jump out of a careening wagon to escape. She would likely injure herself; he could easily overtake her. So she held on for dear life.

He cursed harshly then looked at her. "Forgive the language, my dear, that wasn't fit for a lady's ears. I'm afraid that we must stop at the river ahead and lose this cumbersome wagon. It's slowing down our flight."

Erica blinked in nervous astonishment, his apology, his smile, his very manner seeming to belong to another man.

Once they broke through the trees and he reined in the horses, Erica spoke the words she feared to know: "Where are you taking me?"

He jumped down and moved toward the horses.

"Alaska. I never planned to travel so far north, but I

think it wise. We can easily lose ourselves in such country."

Erica shook her head. "But why take me? Why not just leave me here?"

He momentarily stopped his task and looked at her as if shocked she should ask. "What sort of man would I be to leave a woman out here all alone?"

She shook her head in absolute disbelief, his lackadaisical attitude to the whole sordid affair sharpening her angst. "What sort of man? You held a gun on me! You hit me and tried to kill Christopher. You *did* kill your father! And for what? Money?"

He narrowed his eyes and detached the harness from one side.

"You don't understand the whole story, Miss Chandler. I wouldn't hurt you…" He glanced at her again. "And I *am* terribly sorry about your face. It won't happen again. And Christopher?" He chuckled. "Well, I didn't kill him, now did I? But he *did* turn on me and would have told my father our plan. You heard." His eyes welled with sorrow. "Why would he do that?" he asked as if he didn't really know. "We were friends."

"He was trying to help you," she breathed, feeling disassociated from reality as she watched his bizarre emotions change to yet another facet of the extreme.

"Well, it doesn't matter anymore." He moved around to the other side. "I'll give you all you could ever desire. You'll soon discover that wealth can buy anything on this earth, and I have plenty. We shall forge a happy life together. We'll build a fine house, the finest in the land. I'll buy you dresses and furs and jewels, whatever your heart desires. And as Mrs. Jake Millstone, you'll have the respect of all you meet."

She stared at him in horrified fascination as he spun his twisted fairy tale.

"I never said I would marry you."

"But why would you not? I'm handsome, I'm wealthy and established, and I can love you as you've never been loved before."

"You speak to me *of love*? You're a murderer!"

He gave a careless shrug. "There aren't many men in these parts who haven't taken the life of another, for whatever reason. I'm just one of that number. You'll soon forget what happened today and will learn to enjoy your new life in Alaska. The land is beautiful and rugged and wild, so I hear. You have the spirit to survive there."

"I like it here."

"But I told you, my dear, we need to hide. They'll be looking for us." As he spoke in patient explanation, he moved to where she sat, offering his hand to help her down. She craned away, thinking to slide to the other side, but his hands grasped her waist with a little laugh.

"Such a feisty thing, you are," he said in approval, lifting her from the wagon as if she weighed next to nothing and setting her in front of him. "It's what drew me to you. Your determination to get what you want no matter the odds. I've never met a woman like you. I can't wait to make you my wife."

To her shock, he bent and tenderly kissed her cheek.

With both hands at his chest, Erica pushed him away hard and turned, taking a few steps from him. His laughter followed.

"We're a lot alike, you know. I do what I must to get all I desire, too."

Her hands went to her anger-flushed cheeks and she stared ahead. She now knew without a doubt, the man was stark-raving mad. He didn't even seem to understand that what he'd done was wrong, and it was impossible to reason with him.

Her eye caught a stir in the trees, and she held her breath, her heart beating fast... She hoped her abductor had not seen and turned again, acting as a distraction. She walked past him a short distance then whirled to face him. As she hoped, he turned fully to look at her.

"But how can I marry you when I know so little about you?" she appealed, hoping that she sounded as if she actually considered the possibility.

"We'll have a lifetime to get to know each other."

She feigned a bashful laugh. "That's not how we do things where I come from."

"Oh? Then how do you do them? Oregon isn't exactly a world away from Washington. Surely it can't be much different from where I lived."

His manner was jovial, light and engaging, and she saw how he could win the ladies with his charm, those who didn't know the foul truth of his character. Outwardly, he seemed like the sort that the handsome heroes of her novels were fashioned after, but inwardly his soul was as black as tar.

Her heart leaped as Christopher silently emerged from the trees, rifle in hand, and she kept her attention fixed on their enemy lest he become suspicious.

She recalled what Nora told her. "Well, there should be a proper amount of courting, and after a few weeks, I might let you hold my hand." She smiled shyly.

She should have joined the stage like her mother.

"I can't wait weeks for you, Erica, though I won't dishonor you. I'll wait for you until we're wed."

She blinked again in absolute confusion. Who was this man? He hardly seemed what she knew him to be, what he admitted to be with his own lips: a heartless murderer.

A greedy monster. She wondered what had made him the way he was, and in that moment she pitied him.

His eyes suddenly opened wider as the barrel of Christopher's rifle met with Jake's back.

"One move," Christopher said low and fierce, "and I'll blow you to kingdom come. Lift your hands in the air."

Sadness mixed with anger flickered in Jake's eyes as he complied and looked at Erica. "So, you betray me, too? We could have had a good life, Erica… ."

She stared at him in confusion, his outrageous words, that he actually believed them robbing her of speech.

"Get his guns," Christopher ordered her quietly.

She broke from her daze, first retrieving her Derringer from Jake's coat pocket and slipping it back into her boot top before taking both his gun and Christopher's from his holsters. Uncertain what to do with them, she held them.

"Give them to me," Christopher ordered her.

With his hands on the rifle, she moved around him and slipped the guns into his holsters, feeling a measure of reassurance as she stood close to him, his warmth comforting the chill that had infused her skin since Jake first abducted her from town.

"Move!" Christopher ordered Jake with a jab of his rifle. "Turn around and face me. I won't shoot a man in the back."

Jake did as ordered, his hands in the air.

"There's some rope in the wagon," Erica offered. "I'll get it."

"That won't be necessary."

At Christopher's low retort, Erica blinked, curious then horrified as she saw him reach for his handgun and toss the rifle away from him.

Jake gave a hollow laugh. "It wasn't even loaded, was it?"

"This one is." Christopher cocked the hammer and took

two steps, aiming it at Jake's head. Jake fell to his knees, and Christopher pressed the barrel into Jake's brow.

"Christopher! No...you can't do this."

Erica's voice came hoarse with the realization that Christopher intended to go through with his plan of revenge. And she prayed with all that was within her for help in stopping him.

Burning hatred mixed with rage boiled within Christopher's blood, his sole focus on the gun aimed at the middle of Jake's forehead, where tiny beads of sweat had popped out. His every attention rested on his finger ready at the trigger.

"Christopher, please..."

Erica's voice, soft and gentle, remained the only influence that prevented him from squeezing the thin sliver of metal to finish off this vermin. His memories taunted him to recall the fire, his face, the grisly murders—along with every despicable thing Jake had ever been guilty of doing.

"He doesn't deserve to live," Christopher said to Erica, never taking his grim eyes from his objective. "You don't know the half of what he's done."

How long he had waited for this day! For more than a year, he had planned, tracked down his enemy, all the while hiding from everyone, living like an animal...because of *this man* shaking on his knees before him. This man who had lived like a king. Who had gotten away with every evil lie and wrongdoing since boyhood, sometimes pinning the blame on Christopher. The sight of Jake's fear unhinged a deeper degree of cold satisfaction. He should be made to pay, be made to suffer for each crime he'd ever committed and gotten away with...

"Please, spare me," Jake whispered.

"*Spare you?* Like you did me? Like you spared your

father?" Determined, Christopher kept his aim steady, though his finger felt paralyzed, unable to take that last step.

"You're not like this," Erica insisted. "This is not who you are."

Christopher clenched his teeth through the rage. "This is all I've wanted for *over a year*! Since I woke up from the fire!"

"And I understand that, I do. After what he did to you, I understand it so much more… But sometimes what we think we want isn't really where our heart's desire lies." She stepped a short piece in front of him.

He refused to look at her.

"Christopher, you're a good man. You were raised a godly man."

"God doesn't want anything more to do with me," he snapped.

"That's where you're wrong. He's never forsaken you. Men are to blame for that."

"I don't want to talk about God," he insisted, her soft, relentless words bringing up the memory of his saintly mother and her solemn instruction to him that day of their last picnic. He felt the sting of moisture film his eyes and disgustedly blinked it away, noting his arm had begun to tremble. He brought his other hand up to hold it steady. "It's better if you turn around, Erica. You don't need to see this."

Instead, she stepped closer. At the gentle touch of her hand on his sleeve, another wave of weakness rushed through him.

"Christopher, this is cold-blooded murder. This isn't you. You're a noble man at heart. Everything you've done since we met proves that. But if you do this, it makes you no better than he is."

"This isn't murder," he insisted, "this is justice!"

"The law doesn't see it that way. My *father* won't see it that way."

At her quiet rejoinder he briefly closed his eyes and shook his head.

"Please, Christopher…don't throw away your life in the second it takes to pull that trigger. You have the chance to gain it all back, to live *free* again."

"My life can never go back to being what it was," he insisted angrily, using his shoulder to swipe at the tear that had broken free of his lashes and mask to graze his jaw.

"No, it can't," she agreed. "But it can be better than before. You'll never know if you continue down this path of vengeance. You'll suffer the punishment, just like *he* will if you let him live." He heard the desperation in her voice. "Please, Christopher. *Please* don't do this to yourself. Please don't…for me?" Her last words came softer, uncertain but full of hope.

Hope.

Again, she offered him a line of hope. His resolve wavered, but he wasn't sure he had the strength to grab hold and pull himself from the mire of despair and doubt he had lived in for so long. His mind replayed her words.

Nothing he could do would change the past. A bullet to Jake's brain might give fleeting satisfaction, but he doubted it would ease the ache of years of torment. It wouldn't give him back the life lost to him. His face. His home. It wouldn't mend the endless string of wrongs done.

Killing Jake would accomplish nothing in setting things right.

But it *would* end what little life Christopher had struggled to keep and destroy all hope of a future. On earth. After death…

His gaze flicked to Erica, the first time Christopher had allowed himself to meet her eyes since she tied his hands as ordered and left him physically bound. Now she sought to strip him of his vengeful will, which was far worse. For more than a year, the bitterness was all that held him together in his darkness.

Her glowing eyes beseeched his, full of fear and hope, regret and yearning. Her tears reminded him of dewdrops. Shimmering in her eyes. Thickening her lashes with moisture. Raining softly down her cheeks…

"*Please*," she whispered.

His arm unsteady, Christopher slowly lowered the gun and took a step back. His body felt instantly drained of all energy, his heart and mind weary and uncertain.

"Get the rope," he whispered.

Erica hurried to obey, noting that Christopher never again looked at her. He tied Jake's hands and feet then threw him into the back of the wagon. When Jake resisted, beginning to curse at the reality that his stretch of time as a wealthy tycoon was over, Christopher took the scarf that Erica had bound his hands with and gagged Jake. Without glancing at her, Christopher ordered Erica to keep her gun trained on their prisoner and again hitched up the wagon, fetching his horse and tying it behind.

Erica covertly watched Christopher, anxious he might still change his mind and eager to get to the jailhouse so they could be rid of Jake. But above that, she was concerned. Christopher had not spoken a word to her after his concise orders. Throughout the drive he remained stoic and distant, staring straight ahead.

In frustration, Erica wondered if he resented her for stopping his hand. Well, let him. One day, she hoped soon, he would realize that she had intervened on his behalf. She ached to tell him of the feelings so carefully tucked inside her. A fragile piece in the discovery of who she was and what he meant to her that made her anxious but hopeful. Would he see them as something to be desired?

Glancing at his taciturn features, and with their enemy bound and gagged as a third party witness, she decided now was not the time for such revelations.

Their entry into town brought outright stares from those on the main street. Men and women alike trickled from inside buildings, their reactions curious and amazed. Erica felt more than a modicum of satisfaction to see the workers of *The Chronicle* gaping like fish as the wagon trundled past, their eyes going to Erica and her masked man, who was clearly no fantasy of her imagination, then to Jake lying bound and gagged in the back.

Her father exited the jailhouse, Ralph in his wake. The surprise etched on their faces to see the trio made Erica realize her disappearance must have gone undiscovered.

"Erica?" Her father looked from Christopher, clearly recognizing him even with the mask from the way his brows lifted in surprise, then to Jake, trussed up in the back like a turkey and glaring at everyone. "I wondered why you didn't come back at noon but figured you had business in town and forgot…" His words trailed off as he glanced at Christopher again, shaking his head a little in confusion, then turned to look at Erica.

"I thought the meeting was to be private?"

"We ran into some complications."

"We?" Pointedly he looked at Christopher.

Christopher stepped down from the wagon and faced her father. "I imagine I have no need to tell you my name, Sheriff," he began, his voice wary but determined. "However, I can tell you something you don't know. That fiend in the back of the wagon is the man I was presumed to have murdered a year and a half ago. His real name is Jake Miller. And as you can see, he's very much alive."

Erica's heart pounded as she observed the two men she cared most about in the world eyeing each other and on their guard.

Ralph glanced back and forth from Jake to Christopher, as if unsure who to arrest.

"I didn't kill him; I didn't kill his father. But he did try to kill Erica after he abducted her."

Her father's eyes widened in shock. Instantly he looked her way.

"You all right, honey?"

"I'm fine, Papa." She stepped down from the wagon, not failing to note Ralph's sudden surprise at hearing Christopher's informal use of her name. He swung his gaze to her, again to Christopher, then briefly dropped his focus to the ground, clearly ill at ease at what had just been exposed.

Her father instantly stepped into his role. "Let's take this inside. Deputy, if you would escort the prisoner to his new cell."

Erica moved to follow, but her father stopped her. "It would be best if you stayed here."

"But—" She blinked in concern, her gaze darting to Christopher's. He was staring at her, his expression hard to define.

"Don't worry, Erica. I'm not going to toss him in a cell and throw away the key. You wanted us to talk, remember?"

"Yes. But I thought I would be there when you did."

"Not this time. I sense a lot of hostility between those two, and there's no telling what kind of language might be aired."

As if she hadn't heard cursing in the streets before. "Papa, really, I'm not a child."

"No, but you're my daughter and a lady. And while you're under my roof I intend to see that you're protected if it's within my ability to do so. Something I sadly neglected in the past, and your mother wouldn't be one bit happy about that. *Neither* of them would."

Erica saw how important this was to him and gave a reluctant nod. "All right. But I'll be right here, waiting."

"I don't doubt that."

In frustration, she watched Christopher follow Ralph and the bound and gagged Jake inside, her father joining them. She wished she could be there to speak on Christopher's behalf, but she trusted her father to do the right thing. Above that, she trusted her heavenly Father to pave a way where there seemed not to be one. Less than an hour ago, she feared that she would be trapped in Alaska and might never see her loved ones again. God had saved her from captivity, through Christopher. And Himself once a captive so all could be free, she reminded herself, He could save Christopher in this situation, too.

She prayed a silent prayer of thanks for their safe return, followed by a petition for Christopher's complete absolution from guilt.

Surely all would be well now…

For all her assurances, Erica could not keep from pacing, a slow, silent trek. She ignored the several curious bystanders who lingered in the street to watch.

"Peace, Lord," she muttered under her breath. "I need peace. Please give me peace…"

"Miss Chandler?"

She turned to Mr. Aldridge, who hurried her way.

"You promised we could have that talk," he said by way of greeting. "I looked for you earlier but couldn't find you."

She regarded him in disbelief. Was the man unaware of the commotion throughout town upon her and Christopher's arrival? Had he missed all of it?

"Of course, Mr. Aldridge, how may I be of help?"

"I beseech you to reconsider your current course of action."

She blinked at him. "I'm sorry, *what* course of action?"

He winced and wrung his hands in front of him as if about to make a grave confession. "Your, *ahem*," he cleared his throat, "association with Mr. Millstone. I realize we're not well acquainted, but you seem like a young woman of principles, and Jake Millstone is not an honorable man. I came upon him in his room talking to himself, as it were, and hoarding a great deal of money in a satchel. Naturally, upon seeing this, I was astonished and suspicious, more so when Mr. Millstone stashed the rolls of bills away upon seeing me, with a rather tepid excuse of having recently sold land. Upon a whim, I decided to form an acquaintanceship to see what more I could learn. He revealed matters of a most appalling nature. Shocking crimes of his past. Later, he revealed more. He spoke of your," again he coughed awkwardly, "mutual interest and told me you were eloping with him."

Erica could not contain a gasp of outraged surprise. "I assure you, Mr. Aldridge, any thoughts of pursuing a relationship were entirely on Mr. Millstone's part. I have no interest in him, but I am extremely interested to hear more of your story."

For the next few minutes, Erica listened intently to all Mr. Aldridge said. Excitement bubbled within her. "Would you mind speaking to my father about this? He's in the jailhouse now, with Mr. Millstone in custody. I think your story has bearing on what is going on in there at this very moment."

Mr. Aldridge glanced timidly at the jailhouse. "I suppose I could…"

"Thank you so much, Mr. Aldridge," she enthused and boldly took hold of his arm, moving with him in that direction, afraid he would change his mind and run. "Believe me, your story is sure to help matters."

"Miss Chandler, a word please…"

At the familiar voice she almost groaned. Was this a test?

She turned in puzzled frustration then nodded for Mr. Aldridge to go ahead. "I'll be there shortly."

"Mr. Nilsson," she said warily as the journalist approached.

"That was Jake Millstone tied up in the wagon, wasn't it? And your masked man?"

"You mean the one who doesn't exist?"

He winced. "Yes, well, perhaps we were too hasty. I'd like to hear your story of what happened here today and how it involves Mr. Millstone."

She cast a disinterested look at the pencil he produced along with the piece of paper from his pocket. He unfolded it to a blank side in preparation to write. When she said nothing, he looked up at her in question.

"You may tell your editor that if he wishes for the story, I will be the one to supply the article. Otherwise, I cannot help you. Now, if you'll excuse me?" She smiled politely, knowing by his uneasy expression that she had at last gained the upper hand, and turned to enter the jailhouse with a little sense of triumph.

Her father didn't act surprised to see her as he turned slightly from Mr. Aldridge, who was telling his story. Erica shrugged apologetically, the desire to know the facts too strong. Jake Millstone sat on a cot inside one of two prison cells, his back to them. The deputy stared at Christopher's image on the wall. Christopher stood nowhere in sight, and she assumed he must be in the back room.

She walked toward Ralph. He turned to her, his eyes kind but sad.

"I never had a chance, did I?" His voice came low so as not to be overheard.

She had never wanted to hurt him. "The heart can't decide. It just knows."

He seemed puzzled, and she smiled, his reaction a sure sign that she'd made the right choice. It was the first they'd spoken of matters outright and personal, but it didn't upset her. On her part, the unease had faded now that he understood they could only be friends.

"One day, you'll remember my words, Ralph, and will know what I mean. You'll see that girl, and your heart will know it's found its other half, that you're incomplete without each other."

He wistfully nodded. "I hope so, Erica."

She watched as he took down the wanted poster, and then she looked around the room again.

Christopher had not returned.

"Where is he?" she asked, not needing to elaborate.

"He left."

"Left?"

A hollow ache filled Erica's chest.

And her heart knew.

Chapter 13

Christopher stared at the distant ribbon of river, not sure how long he'd been standing there. With a weary sigh, he turned back to camp, knowing the time had come.

It was over.

The hunt. The escape. The hiding.

Over…

The reality had not yet formed in his mind, and he wasn't sure if anything had really changed. The law might no longer be chasing him, but still he couldn't live among others, his future destined to be one of solitude. He had been given a second chance, but to what purpose?

Halfway through his packing, he heard the rustle in the bushes. He didn't need to turn around to know she was there.

"Why did you leave without saying good-bye?" she asked after some time passed.

He tugged hard on the rope, finishing the knot. Still not looking at her, he hoisted his bedroll, tying it to his horse.

"You're leaving?" Her voice came softer, a trace of hurt there.

No longer able to fight the urge to look at her, Christopher glanced her way. "Why did you come?"

"I…to tell you that my father said he'll see to it that the bounty is removed from your head. He's sending a telegraph to both the mayor and the governor. You're cleared of all blame, Christopher."

Silent, he stared, certain she would know that her father had already shared the news with him and wondering why she had really come. She fidgeted under his unswerving look and nervously averted her gaze. He took a moment to admire her beauty, the light that always seemed to glow in her expressive eyes and shine from her hair and skin.

Swiftly he turned to the task of filling his knapsack.

"Thank you for telling me, Erica. And…for everything else you've done."

After over a year of striving for one thing and letting go when it was within his grasp, Christopher felt emptied, wearied, but beneath it all, there existed a layer of gratitude that he had not gone through with killing a man. He had her to thank for that.

But after over one month of finding hope for love again, no matter how futile, and seeing it dissolve with the whisking away of his mask, he felt lost, his heart again battered.

"Why are you leaving?"

"I can't stay here." He closed his knapsack.

"No, of course not." She sounded chagrined. "Are you getting a room in town?"

"No. I'm leaving for good."

"Oh." He wondered if he imagined the disappointment in her voice. "You're going back home?"

He shook his head and stood. "There's nothing left for me in Oregon."

"Then why leave?" she insisted. "You're no longer wanted. There's no longer any reason to hide."

"Isn't there?" he asked wryly and again gave in to the painful lure to look at her.

She was so beautiful. Her skin like cream and roses, her hair lustrous, her voice like silk. If God ever created an earthly angel, she could be His inspiration.

Her eyes seemed brighter than usual. She clasped her hands in front of her, looking as lost as he felt.

"And were you just going to leave without saying goodbye?" Her voice came quiet. "I thought that you…that *we* had reached an understanding. After that night, when you came to my house—" She broke off, her cheeks flushed.

Surprised she would bring it up, he looked away. "Forget that night, Erica. Forget me."

"Why?"

There was no mistaking the tears in her voice.

"What if I don't want to forget you, Christopher?"

"It's best that you do. I may no longer be wanted, but that changes nothing. I have no trade, no job…."

"It shouldn't be hard for a man like you to find one."

"I have no home."

"Not insurmountable. That, too, can change."

"But there are some things that cannot change." He shook his head and sadly smiled at her. "You deserve more than half a man, Erica."

She gasped. Determination firmed her small shoulders, at the same time realization of what he just admitted entered his weary mind. Christopher turned fully away, unwilling to draw out the heartache further. Grabbing his rifle, he fastened it to his saddle. He wished she would go and make this easier on both of them. At the same time, he seized every last stealthy glimpse of her he could take with him to remember her by.

Erica wondered why she hadn't realized the truth sooner. Perhaps because what mattered so strongly to Christopher did nothing to alter her perception of him.

He was the kindest, the bravest, the strongest man she'd ever met. To suffer through all he had and still put others first—it astonished her. He might fight it, deny it, might be angry and embittered because of it, but in the end he always chose an altruistic path, ever since she'd first met him.

Looking into his smoky green eyes, she could see the sorrow and hopelessness there that had never left, contrary emotions to his newfound freedom, and at last she felt she understood the presence of such feelings. His wounds ran deeper than having been accused unjustly, deeper than losing all he once owned. Deeper even than the great amount of physical anguish he had endured.

And those unseen wounds were the true barriers that separated them.

But she had seen. He knew she had seen. And now he was running, afraid of what else he might witness in her eyes.

At first, she did know shock and horror. The shock of the truth, the horror of all he had suffered, and the severity of his scars had twisted her stomach into a knot of pain. But it didn't alter the way she felt about the man behind the mask.

She wanted to tell him all this but couldn't frame intelligible words, her heart pounding so strongly as she watched him prepare to leave her life for good.

"I want you to stay," she said quietly, then more firmly when he went motionless. "I want you to stay."

He shook his head, his back turned to her. "I can't."

"Why?"

She watched his shoulders tense, silently begging him to speak, to not throw away whatever this was that existed between them before they had a chance to find out.

"It would be too difficult." His voice came low, harsh, full of emotion as if he spoke through clenched teeth.

"What would be too difficult?" she pressed softly and took a tentative step toward him.

He shook his head again as if disgusted.

"What would be too difficult, Christopher?" Her voice came in a near wisp of breath as she moved even closer.

He spun to face her, and she halted her slow advance in surprise. His jaw contorted with rage and hurt.

"You want to strip me of any morsel of pride I have left? You want me to speak what's burning in my heart? Fine. You. It would be too difficult to be near you." Moisture glimmered in his eyes, and his throat worked hard, forcing down emotion. "To see you all the time, to be so close and never be able to have—" His words ended abruptly, and he clenched his jaw.

"Never be able to have what?"

He looked at her incredulously.

"Christopher…" She felt suddenly shy, but the knowledge that she could lose him forever propelled her tongue. "Do you care for me?"

He let out a short laugh devoid of humor. "You really don't know?"

She shook her head. "This, what we have shared this past month, is all new to me. Before you, I had never been kissed…."

He looked away, a flush darkening what skin she could see.

"I've never let anyone kiss me," she whispered, praying not to lose her courage now when it mattered most. "I never wanted to…before you."

Slowly, she moved toward him. His head snapped up, his eyes wary.

"I care," she told him quietly.

He blinked, and she watched a tear fall to the soft leather eyehole and become absorbed there. "How can you, now that you know?" His question came hoarse as she stopped before him.

"Because there is so much more to you"—her fingers lifted to the edge of his mask, and he flinched—"than this."

"Don't, Erica." His hand grabbed hers to stop her, his plea a broken whisper. Something in his helpless, panicked expression gave her the calm strength she needed to unmask all of what lay in her heart.

Gently she slipped her fingers from his hold and brought his hand to her mouth.

Christopher stared in shock as she tenderly, almost reverently kissed his hand, letting her caress linger. At the touch of her lips on his skin, his heart leaped to his throat, pounding there. He felt transfixed by the steady look in her shining brown eyes when she again lifted them to him.

He wanted to flee but felt weak and defenseless, knowing there was nowhere to run. He had finally been granted freedom, but never had he felt more trapped.

She gradually lifted her left hand, still holding with her right one his hand she had kissed.

"Please, no," he rasped.

"Why?" she questioned yet again, bringing that hand to clasp his as well, the answers she continually sought agonizing and impossible to explain. But he found those defenses had crumbled with the press of an angel's lips.

"I don't want you to despise me." His voice cracked. In vain he blinked back the hot moisture coating his eyes. "I've suffered a lot, Erica, but I couldn't bear that."

"Foolish man," she said lightly, tears rimming her own eyes. "I could never despise you."

"You could. It's happened before."

"Trust me, Christopher. Please…trust my heart…"

She released his hand, and he felt her fingers tremble against his cheek, whether in fear or dread, he didn't want to know. Feeling suddenly drained and powerless to stop her but no less terrified, he closed his eyes, loath to see the disgust and revulsion that would surely be present there, a repeat of all that Carla had shown toward him.

The mask that shielded the destruction of his every dream slipped gently from his face, the cool air rushing to bathe his damp skin. He squeezed his eyes tighter, his hands clenching into nervous fists when she made no sound. No little shriek, no gasp. Nothing. And the silence tore through him. His chest ached as if his heart had been hollowed out. Desperately he tried to come up with some sarcastic quip to mask the pain and give him the courage to open his eyes and face her.

"Not very pretty, is it?" The nonchalance he tried for fell flat. "I can never change this. Can never be like Jake or your deputy friend—"

"Thank God for that," she whispered.

His eyes flew open at the rush of her warm breath on his ravaged skin, and he gave a hoarse little cry when her cool lips brushed his twisted cheek. She pulled away a few inches.

"Did I hurt you?" she asked fearfully.

He could barely shake his head no, then froze in confusion when she cradled his face between her soft hands and resumed pressing slow, delicate kisses to his reddened, shiny scars, catching his tears with the blessing of her lips.

"I don't want your pity," he whispered, his body trembling harder.

"Then you shan't have it." She kissed his ridged temple and the small patch on his forehead where the hair no longer grew. Her touch felt like fire and ice, sweet tingles of warmth and chill, a comfort to skin that had known only distress and pain.

"It's enough to know that you're not re-repulsed by me. You—you don't have to do this." He could barely get the words out, the tears now flowing freely, though he desperately tried to quench them.

She brushed her lips tenderly over the several sparse hairs that made up his right eyebrow then pulled back to look into his eyes. Her face shone with her own tears, her eyes bright and glowing with an emotion he feared to name.

"Maybe I want to."

Before he could reply, she lightly pressed her lips to his.

Christopher grabbed her wrists hard...

But he didn't push her away.

The sweet warmth that saturated Erica as she gave in to her heart blossomed while something inside Christopher broke. His strong arms wrapped about her, pulling her swiftly to him, the pressure of his lips powerful and insistent. She moved her hands from his jaw to clutch his shoulders, feeling her world begin to spin with the passion of his kiss, her body trembling with a myriad of emotions as much as his did, the salt of tears that wet her mouth a mingling of their shared release of fear...

With a harsh sob, he broke away. Grabbing her shoulders, he hung his head, and she experienced more compassion than she had known existed as he gasped for breath, his sobs racking the air, then dropped to his knees as if the weight of his feelings were impossible to endure.

Her own tears never ceasing, Erica also dropped to her knees and drew him to her shoulder, holding him like a babe as he wept and released inconceivable heartache and pain. His arms gripped her tightly, desperately.

She brushed her lips against his head then pressed her cheek against his hair, holding him close.

"I'm here," she whispered. "I'm here…" Quietly she began to hum a little song of hope.

And she knew, in that moment, without any of her previous doubts, that *with him* was where she would always remain.

Chapter 14

Erica finished her hymn, afterward quietly stepping down from the podium.

Sweet, reverent silence filled the air, but every face turned toward her shone with restrained delight and overwhelming peace. Grateful to have been the vessel to instill such emotion, still only one man's opinion really mattered to her, and taking a seat beside him while looking into his beautiful eyes, she smiled at his reaction.

Christopher reached for her hand, covering it with his. She turned hers so that their palms met and entwined her small fingers with his long, slender ones.

"I once thought God had abandoned me," he whispered so only she could hear. "But I know now instead He sent an angel to help me through a very bad time and find my way back to Him. With a voice like that, you could be nothing else."

Heat warmed her face, but she couldn't prevent a pleased smile.

"Hush, deputy, or they'll hear. Preacher's about to speak."

He gave her hand a gentle squeeze, releasing it, and Erica breathed a little distressed sigh to lose his warmth as she primly returned her hand to her lap. She longed for the day when they could be man and wife and such public gestures wouldn't be frowned upon; that is, if Christopher ever asked...

Months had passed, now long into autumn, since that early summer afternoon when their lives dramatically changed. During the weeks her father transported Jake back to Oregon and the authorities there, Ralph had agreed to postpone his trip home, and to Erica's surprised pleasure, he and Christopher became good friends. Her own relationship with Ralph had deepened, to thinking of him as an older brother, and it was with a heavy heart she told him good-bye, promising to write. While the change in feeling all of them had toward one another astonished her, she had not been the least bit surprised when her father offered Christopher the vacant spot of his deputy. He also had seen Christopher's courage and strength of character, and Erica could not be more pleased.

Well, there was one thing that could make her happier...

Her eyes drifted from the face of the man she loved over to Nora, who sat on the other side of Christopher. Her third mother caught her eye and shook her head in mild rebuke. Only slightly chagrined, with a little smile Erica turned her eyes back to the preacher and fully concentrated on his message.

After the church meeting, once they stepped outside, Christopher grabbed her arm and pulled her away from the emerging crowd. His eyes gleamed behind the mask, making her wonder. Noting it was askew, she lifted her hand to tug the material gently in place.

Because his scars were so sensitive to sunlight, to the point of pain, he'd told her it was necessary to wear the mask. Erica thought he hid a different reason but didn't insist. He had already come so far, and the road to healing could be a lengthy one. The townspeople had long stopped giving him odd stares and had accepted him as one of their own. He was a respected member of society, proving his worth as a deputy and a friend at every turn. She doubted, even if he walked among them without his mask, that they would react any differently. But he thought so, and she let the matter drop the first time they spoke of it. Only inside her home, when he visited for meals, and every evening they spent together, did he give in to Erica's customary request that he remove the covering, to give his skin relief from the constant rub of leather.

"Before we join Nora and your father on the picnic, there's somewhere I'd like to take you," Christopher said. "Will you come?"

"Of course." She smiled.

Did he truly need to ask? She would follow him anywhere. Even if it meant leaving her hometown, should her dream of a life with him ever occur, she would gladly do that, too.

"Miss Chandler?"

She turned as Mr. Nilsson hurried toward her, a letter outstretched in his hand. "This came for you yesterday after you left."

"Thank you." She took the envelope, noting the postmark immediately.

"Glad to help. I'll see you tomorrow." He tipped his hat and walked away.

"Yes, of course," she said vaguely.

Since her article on Jake's capture, she had received the long-awaited respect of those at *The Chronicle*, including the hard-nosed editor, who gruffly offered her a position, admitting she "had something." What that something was, he never clarified, but that he had pushed aside his traditional views and given her the desired chance she considered a great triumph. He was still hard-nosed, that had not changed, but Erica had long been accustomed to his gruff mannerisms.

Now, staring at the envelope, she felt a rush of dizziness and grabbed Christopher's sleeve.

"Erica?" he said in alarm. "Angel, what's wrong?"

She shook her head, unable to reply, and he wrapped a supportive arm around her, escorting her to a wagon. So overwhelmed by the implications of the simple piece of paper in her hand, she barely noticed that the conveyance was her father's. She gave Christopher a curious look as he helped her to her seat.

"He said we could borrow it for a spell." Quickly he moved to the driver's side and settled down beside her. "Now, tell me. What has you behaving so strangely?"

At the concern in his voice, she held up the letter.

"It's from my father. The—the one in California."

His arm tightened around her shoulders, his other hand clasping hers. She felt grateful for his warmth and leaned into him, soaking up his strength.

"Are you going to open it?" His tone came light, reassuring. "You'll tie yourself in a bundle of nerves if you put it off…. If you'd rather do it in private—"

"No." She clutched his fingers fiercely. "I want you to stay."

With trembling hands, Erica opened the letter.

Shortly after she joined *The Chronicle*, she used her new position to locate her father, learning he was alive.

After weeks of conflicting emotions, she drummed up enough courage to write him. Months passed, an entire season, without the response she had resigned herself never to receive.

> *Dear Erica,*
> *To say I was shocked to receive your missive would be a gross understatement. I am frankly surprised that anyone would tell you about me, after the despicable way in which I behaved....*

The letter went on to give his account of leaving the wagon train, briefly showing her the grief he suffered and his inability to think with any reason at the time. He further stated that with his prospect of the future dead along with her mother, instead of purchasing a partnership in the opera house as had been his intent, he took to heavy gambling and lost all he had. He tried different lines of work, none of them theatrically related, only to subsist. His grief never letting up, work became too much of a struggle, and he chose to give up living. An old miner found him alone and starving in the woods and practically bullied him back to health, telling him he had no right to end his life since he didn't start it, and the only one with the right to choose was the one who began it.

> *The man was a menace. I barely could tolerate his company, but he wouldn't give up on me. Your dear mother was a godly woman. She loved to sing and had exquisite talent, not at all loose or tawdry as those of society choose to call those of us who work in a thespian profession. I heard her words echoed in that old miner's—his coarse, but with the same message—and for the first time I began to listen and*

*apply them to myself. I believe that despite my er-
rors in this life, and there have been many, God has
forgiven my weaknesses and transgressions. With
all humility I beseech you to do the same. It was
difficult to look upon your sweet face, so much like
my Sarah's, but I did love you. I was mad with grief
and had no idea how to take care of an infant; but
even in my temporal insanity, I knew that you would
be well looked after and find a better life than anything I could give. It behooves me to write this, but
letting you go was perhaps the one unselfish thing
I have done.*

 *Thank you for writing to me. It gives my soul
peace it has missed to know that you are alive and
well.*

Erica's tears fell silently, and Christopher's knuckle
gently nudged her chin his way.

"Are you all right?" he asked in concern.

"He loved me," she said simply, all of her long-held
ideas of why her father left shattered with the scrawl of a
few sentences.

"How could he help but do anything else?" he whispered. Then glancing at a few children who Erica also
now noticed curiously stared their way, he took the reins
and drove the wagon out of town.

Her heart beat in time with the hoofbeats as she pondered Christopher's words again and again. He had never
come right out and told her that he loved her, though he'd
shown his affection in a number of small ways. Holding her
hand. A gentle touch. Sweet words. After that last passionate, emotional kiss they shared when she first unmasked
him, he never instigated another of such depth. His kisses
were now brief and chaste, often to her cheek in farewell

and rarely to her lips. She should be relieved not to court temptation, recalling her uncomfortable talk with Nora months before, and leave it at that. But she worried that he'd lost interest in her, or perhaps he never had a wealth of it to begin with, while her affection for him grew with the passage of each new day as Erica realized more and more what it meant to love. Maybe she was foolish, since not everyone married for emotional reasons, but love was a big part of what she wanted. The deep, abiding love her parents had shared. Both her birth parents and her adoptive ones, and she would settle for nothing less.

Her mind in emotional turmoil, going back and forth with doubts about Christopher's true feelings and pondering the letter from her father, she remained silent. At least for once the skies didn't look as if they would dump more rain on their heads, and for that she was grateful.

They came to the hill where it all started, and she looked at him curiously when he jumped down from the wagon, tied the horse, and hurried to her side. Putting his hands to her waist, he lifted her down, their eyes holding for a breathless moment before he took her hand and led her down the path. He brought her around to face him once they stepped into the clearing.

"I've found that after weeks of living in this forest and over a year in others, I prefer solitude to the noisy life in town," he began.

She stared at him in disbelief. "Tell me you're not planning to set up camp in these woods again?"

He chuckled. "Not exactly." He looked toward the river. "Picture a cabin right here, close enough to the water to make use of it, and a window overlooking each sunset. Can you see it, Erica?"

At his excited words, a vision formed in her mind: Christopher fishing with a small green-eyed boy beside him and her tending a garden with a small curly-haired girl. She smiled.

"I see it. But what does it mean?" She felt breathless with hope as she looked into his eyes, which glowed with eagerness. But she sensed nervousness there, too.

"A new life. A new start. I went to the land office yesterday to make arrangements. I want that future you told me I could have. I want it with you."

"With me?" She barely breathed the words.

He took one of her hands in both of his. "I'm asking you to marry me, Erica."

Tears she couldn't restrain welled in her eyes. He frowned.

"You're crying. Don't cry. I…" He dropped his hands from her hand. There was no mistaking his distress. "I thought you felt the same way."

"I thought you didn't want me…that way…anymore." Her answer came faint. "I thought I was only…a friend."

His head hung low, his gaze sweeping the ground. "I'm sorry, Erica. I guess I misunderstood. I shouldn't have spoken."

She grabbed his hand in both of hers, and he looked at her in pained confusion.

"Don't say that. I'm glad you spoke—no, not glad—overjoyed. I've loved you almost since I first set eyes on you, Christopher, but I'd begun to think you didn't feel the same about me."

His eyes widened in disbelief. "How could you ever think that? You're the one who's given me a reason to live again."

"But you've been so distant!"

"Distant?" He shook his head.

"Different than before. The way you treat me. Like a

sister, but not that either. And when we part, the way you kiss me good-bye…"

He gaped at her, and she shook her head in shy embarrassment, suddenly realizing what she'd blurted. "Forget I said that."

"I was trying to behave like a gentleman, something I regret not doing before. And after what I went through with Carla, I was nervous to move forward, afraid in the end you would reject me, too. But you're nothing like her. You're special. A true woman of beauty. Inside and out."

"So you do care about me?"

"*Care about you?*" He shook his head a little in stunned amusement. "Erica, I just asked to *marry you*."

"Oh! You did—so you must love me!" Her smile bright, she threw her arms around his neck, her emotionally drained mind beginning to catch up. "Yes—a thousand times yes, Christopher, I'll marry you, and I already love our cabin near the woods!"

His arms wrapped around her, and he gave her the kiss she'd been dreaming of for months. When he broke from her lips, they were both breathless.

"You asked if I care about you. Do you still doubt it?" he teased.

Clinging to him for fear she might fall, she dazedly shook her head.

"Love seems like such a weak word compared to the depth of all I feel for you." One of his hands lifted to brush through the ringlets at her temple. "You are my life, Erica, the mate of my soul, the beat of my heart. You taught me to live again, to trust. I love everything about you. Your gentle ways. Your eloquent eyes. Your voice…when you sing, it's like streams of pure light reaching down to my soul…"

She inhaled softly, moved by the sincere beauty of his

words. She knew he enjoyed reading literature as much as she did and now wondered if he was a poet, too.

He grinned, a flicker of mischief in his eyes. "...I even love your willful nature and independence, though at times I've been inclined to turn you over my knee."

"Christopher!" Mildly affronted, she made as if to pull away, but he tightened his hold and gave her another kiss, this one tender and wooing. As if she needed to be coaxed!

"You make me feel whole again," he breathed against her lips. "The real question is, how could *you* love *me*?"

She pulled away to look at him and pressed her hand to the soft mask covering the scars beneath. A trace of the old fear clouded his eyes, always struggling to surface.

"You *are* whole. We all have flaws of some sort, and these don't matter to me. You're all I could want. Don't ever think otherwise." One day she prayed that his self-loathing would be banished forever, and she anticipated a shared lifetime to prove her words.

"As awful as it is—what happened to you," she continued softly, "did you ever think that if it hadn't happened, you never would have come to Washington, and we never would have met?" Her lips trembled at such a thought, but she went on: "Likely you would have married Carla, finding out what kind of woman she really is only when it was too late."

"I think about it all the time. It's the only thread of silver in that dark cloud that was my life. You. Always you. You gave me back hope. You *are* my hope. I love you, Erica."

The spires of the stately pines rustled in the wind, a sweet whisper of accompaniment to their vows of shared love. Together, they sat side by side in the spot that would become their home and spoke of the future, the picnic long forgotten.

* * *

Once Christopher drove her home, they found her father and Nora there. They accepted the news of their upcoming nuptials with delight, Erica's father clapping him on the back and calling him son. Nora quickly prepared plates of picnic leftovers for Erica and Christopher, and they spoke more of the wedding and the cabin Christopher would build in the spring. Afterward, Erica sang at her piano, as she often did, pleased that all enjoyed the music, but in her heart, singing only for Christopher.

That night, once she walked outdoors with him and they kissed farewell, through the silver pinpricks of stars above, the dark sky suddenly shimmered and danced with breathtaking streaks of pale green and rose light as it often did at this time of year. They both looked upward in awe.

"It's a sign of hope, Christopher. Of the start of our happy future together."

He smiled. "To know such hope can be granted to me… It's more than I could have ever dreamed possible, Erica."

They watched the heavenly lights of the north, and gently she slipped her arm through his. Resting her head against his strong shoulder, she felt as if they had just received God's personal blessing from above.

Chapter 15

On a bright spring day, when even the birds joined in with their exuberant song, Erica joined her hand to Christopher's and became his wife. It was the most breathless, amazing moment of her life, and in the glow of such bliss, she knew there would never be enough words to describe the extent of all she felt.

Afterward, many relocated to her father's house, where Nora, with Erica's help, had cooked for days. A bountiful feast resulted, with courses both delectable and filling. The night before, Nora shared the talk with Erica as promised but left her with more questions than answers, causing Nora to blush and tell Erica she must learn for herself. Though nervous, she loved Christopher with all her heart, recalling how warm and safe and wonderful she felt when with him, and looked forward to the discovery that would make their union complete.

Among the guests, Erica and Christopher welcomed

her father from California. After his letter, she had not hesitated to write back. A regular stream of communication followed, and the desire to meet had been shared. He had arrived the previous day, and Erica moved toward him now, where he helped himself to a slice of apple pie.

He turned to her, and she studied him. His hair was dark and curly, though not in loose coils like hers. Except for that and his height, Erica being tall for a woman, she saw little else of herself in the man.

"You look so like your mother," he answered her unspoken question with a trace of a European accent, a hint of a waver in his voice. "And I hear you have her talent, too. Will you sing for me before I leave for California next week?"

"Is there a reason you must go back?"

She had thought she would dislike her father after all he'd done. Through the letters, she had forgiven him for abandoning her but still felt uneasy. After meeting him, she changed her mind. Life and the tireless hand of God had mellowed the sharp edges she had been told existed.

"I have no ties there, no, but would you really want me to stay?" Her father's blue eyes regarded her with uncertainty. "I don't want to interfere in your life."

"Yes, I would like you to stay. I've learned that sometimes we all make decisions that later we're not proud of, but learning from them, and the end outcome—that's what's important." She thought of Christopher and his vendetta against Jake. She thought of herself and her reaction to learning she was adopted. "I'd like to know you better. And to learn more about my mother."

He gave her a sad smile, but a twinkle lit his eye. "To write a story? I never suspected my daughter would become a journalist like my father."

"My grandfather was a journalist?" she said in amazement, wondering if she had inherited his thirst always to know more. "I do want to know about him and grand-mother and all those I never knew. But I won't be writing any of it. I'm giving that up."

"I'll think about it," her father agreed. "Maybe this town of yours has some place for an old fool like me. My father wanted me to follow in his footsteps, and for a time I did. Before I decided music was my chosen profession. But I could never go back to the opera…."

Her editor, who'd been standing near a plate of smoked salmon and fish croquettes, suddenly came forward, his eyes on Erica. "I hope I misunderstood what you just said. You're not planning to leave *The Chronicle*?"

Surprised that he should care when he rarely gave her praise, Erica nodded. She had learned there was much more to life than hunting out a good story, which she ini-tially engaged in to escape her loneliness. In her persistent search for one, she had found Christopher, the love of her life and the biggest news to rock their small town in years. She could never top that.

"I had planned to tell you later, but I've decided to turn in my pen so I can fully devote myself to a life with my new husband."

She didn't hear him approach, which came as no sur-prise, but suddenly felt him behind her, his warmth at her back. Without even needing to turn she knew it was Christopher and smiled at the touch of his large hand going to her waist. It was a conundrum. But his presence and strength always made her a little breathless and instilled comfort at the same time.

"I'm sorry to hear that, Mrs. Duvall," Mr. Mahoney said. "If you ever change your mind or have an idea for an article, please, don't hesitate to bring it in."

Erica's smile grew at the sound of her new name, blossomed at her little victory of winning over the editor, and sudden inspiration filled her.

"Mr. Mahoney, I don't believe you've met my father, Mr. Roland Waverly. His father, my grandfather, was also a journalist, and I just learned that my father was one, as well."

"Really?"

Mr. Mahoney shook hands with her father, who flashed Erica an amused, knowing grin. She innocently smiled back.

"Any chance that you will be staying on in Washington?" Mr. Mahoney asked.

"I'll just leave you two gentlemen to talk," she said sweetly, touching her father's arm as she moved away with Christopher.

"That was brilliant manipulation on your part," Christopher said beneath his breath.

She grinned. "I do have my moments."

"How well I know," he said in mock longsuffering, and she laughed. Catching sight of her other father staring out the window, she looked at Christopher. "I should speak with him."

He followed Erica's gaze and nodded.

She raised herself on her toes and kissed his jaw beneath the mask, wishing he didn't feel the need to wear it but respecting his feelings. Among so many, he was nervous without it. With those he felt comfortable around—Erica, her family, and most recently, his friends—he dispensed with the leather covering. It was progress.

She came up beside her father and looked, as he did, out the glass.

"Thank you for all this."

"Of course." He nodded slowly, still not looking at her.

"You know, don't you," she said, hooking her arm

through his and leaning her head against his shoulder, "that you'll always be my father. That will never change."

She sensed his entire body relax. His hand lifted to pat hers.

"I consider myself most fortunate to have had three mothers and two fathers who've cared about me. How many daughters can say that?"

He chuckled. All was quiet for some time as they looked out over the forest of proud and stately conifers and hardwoods, far in the distance, toward the summit of a glacier-capped mountain.

"Erica, I've been thinking. Nora said she must leave once you do, that it wouldn't be proper for her to stay…"

She nodded and waited.

"How would you feel if I officially made her your mother?"

"You mean to propose?"

His skin tinged with red. "Yes."

She giggled. "Then I would say it's about time."

He looked at her in surprise.

"It's no secret how she feels about you. And I know you two have been spending time together lately, so I would hope you feel the same way."

He gave an amused nod. "You knew all along, didn't you?"

"I had hoped. At first I wasn't sure how I felt about it when I suspected, but you two would be good for each other. And she's already part of our family."

"I never thought I could love anyone after your mother." He shook his head softly. "I'm still surprised that I do."

"When will you ask her?"

"Tonight, after the guests leave. If she's agreeable, I thought to marry her next week. Do you think that's too soon?"

She chuckled. "If I know Nora, it won't be soon enough."

She hoped she wasn't betraying Nora by sharing what Erica knew to be true, the love Nora had for her father, but at the relief that suddenly filled his eyes, Erica felt sure she'd made the right choice.

Christopher barely had a chance to speak with his bride and anticipated the moment when they would finally be alone. The sizeable house swarmed with what looked like every face in town, though Christopher doubted all the citizens of Barretts Grove could fit into the rooms.

As he took a drink of sweet cider punch, he caught sight of a familiar face that was no longer a part of their town and watched his friend move toward him.

"Congratulations." Ralph took Christopher's hand and gave it a hearty shake then looked toward Erica, who was in earnest discussion with Nora. "She's the happiest I've ever seen her."

Christopher raised his brow. "Did you doubt she would be?"

"No, not at all… I guess it's no secret to you how I felt."

A twinge of old jealousy gnawed at Christopher. Perhaps it had been a mistake to agree with Erica to write Ralph about their nuptials. "No, it was no secret."

"Rest assured. The better man won. I never had a chance; I see that now."

Ralph's warm, earnest words alleviated the chill, and Christopher smiled.

"It is good to see you again. We were surprised you could come. How are things on the farm?"

"Busy. I have to return tomorrow. It was a challenge at first, going back to working crops, but I managed, and my uncle is there to help now." He grinned. "As a matter of fact, I got engaged."

Christopher looked at him in surprise. "You did?"

"You did?" Erica echoed as she approached and stood beside Christopher, nothing but joy for her friend's news shining in her expressive eyes. "I'm so happy for you, Ralph!"

Christopher relaxed another degree. Erica had proven her love to him a hundred times over, had married him, pledging to be his wife for a lifetime, but still he battled feelings of inferiority due to his scars. Once, though he bore no arrogance in saying it, he'd had a face that could rival any man's. Through Erica's affections, he had learned that looks—good or bad—didn't matter where love was concerned, and she told him often that she thought him quite handsome. He had searched her eyes skeptically each time but never detected anything more than warmth and sincerity. Soon, he stopped searching and took her gentle declarations as fact.

Perhaps beauty really was in the eye of the beholder.

Ralph told them about a childhood companion who had grown into a remarkable woman and quickly caught his heart when he saw her at a social. From that moment he sought her company whenever possible, and she'd eagerly given it. "It turns out, she has loved me since she was six and I was twelve and walked with her to the schoolhouse, due to our farms being so close." The glow in his eyes left no doubt that the man was as besotted with his Megan as Christopher was with his Erica.

After several toasts to the bride and groom, Erica announced she would sing. Christopher took a seat where Nora escorted him, on the sofa nearest Erica. As the older woman turned away, she caught the eye of the sheriff, and for longer than was casual, they stared. She flashed a flustered, girlish smile before moving away.

Christopher silently chuckled. There was definitely something brewing there.

All else ceased to exist as Erica began to sing. Many gaped in wonder at the beauty of her voice. Her birth father stared in amazement, tears running down his cheeks, his eyes holding a faraway gleam as if lost to memories of his Sarah. Erica's bright eyes remained on Christopher throughout her song of love and hope, making clear the feelings in her heart.

Once the song ended, applause filled the room followed by a round of requests.

Erica shook her head politely, and Christopher stepped in and up, sliding his arm around her waist. "I think it's time we left. I want to make it to the cabin before dark." He and several men had worked for weeks to clear the path near the hill and widen it, making it safer for travel by wagon, but he didn't want to take any chances his first night in bringing his bride home. One fall down that hill was enough.

His remark produced a few mildly ribald comments from some of the men. Christopher ignored the usual wedding jests, hoping they wouldn't make Erica nervous. She blushed prettily but smiled at him, no trace of fear in her eyes.

While she made her farewells to her two fathers and Nora, Christopher, Ralph, and two other men moved her small piano into his wagon. Christopher had prepared a special place in the cabin for it to sit, where Erica could stare out the window at the view of the distant river and the sunset beyond the mountain. Once the instrument was tied down, Christopher collected his bride. After a few more farewells, they were finally off to their new home.

Erica eagerly scooted closer to Christopher, looping her arm through his and clutching it.

"I have waited for this day for so long," she said with a happy sigh. "It was everything I hoped it would be." She looked up at him. "You don't need this anymore."

The sun had dipped below the dense cover of trees, and he didn't argue as she untied his mask, feeling a weak lurch in his center as he always did when her lips brushed a scar.

She chattered gaily about the day's events, soon leading him in a game they often shared of citing lines of literature and guessing the authors.

" 'Beauty is bought by judgment of the eye, Not utter'd by base sale of chapmen's tongues,' " she said suddenly.

He threw her a suspicious glance, his lips quirking in amusement.

She giggled. "It really is a line from a book."

"Oh, yes, I recognize it as Shakespeare but cannot think of the title."

"*Love's Labours Lost.*"

Christopher smiled and minutes later inwardly sighed in relief as they made it down the path without difficulty and their cabin appeared in the distance. Ahead, the first stars were just beginning to twinkle above the spires of trees in a twilit sky.

She suddenly went quiet, and he hoped she wasn't apprehensive of this night; in truth, he was also nervous.

"I vow to cherish you for the rest of my days," he whispered to her, and she nodded against his shoulder. "For us, love's labors are newly found, never to be lost." She gave another brief nod, and he suggested something he knew would calm her. "Sing for me, my angel. The song you first sang for me after I met you."

She looked up at him with a nervous grin. "Sing *with* me, Christopher."

Only recently had he sung to her, and she had gaped at him in complete bewilderment then accused him of hiding his talent as well as his face. He had renounced all things past, wishing to forget, due to Carla, who'd often begged him to sing. In embracing this new chance at a future with Erica, a better one than he ever dreamed possible, he was slowly letting go of old fears and reclaiming his identity.

As he guided their wagon homeward, his strong tenor blended with her high soprano in perfect accord, a sweet offering of music to each other, lifting to the heavens above:

Sheaves after sowing, sun after rain,
Sight after mystery, peace after pain;
Joy after sorrow, calm after blast,
Rest after weariness, sweet rest at last.

Near after distant, gleam after gloom,
Love after loneliness, life after tomb;
After long agony, rapture of bliss—
Right was the pathway leading to this.

Epilogue

"Tell us again, Papa, oh, tell us again!" Little Sarah clapped her hands in glee, and Christopher ruffled her dark curls.

"Another time, sweetheart. I'm all worn out."

"Did Mama really aim a gun at you?" Claude chortled. "And fall down the hill and you had to carry her all the way up again?"

"What's this?" Erica came up behind where she had left them almost an hour before, still sprawled on the grassy riverbank. She put her hands to her hips, looking at her husband in mock irritation. "Christopher, just what are you telling the children?"

He deftly moved to his feet. "The story of our life, my dear. Is Baby Elizabeth asleep?"

She nodded and watched Claude pick up his father's discarded mask to tie it around his small face, his green eyes gleaming as he peered through its holes. Christopher only wore the covering in strong sunlight now, to protect his damaged skin, and the thick mass of heavy white clouds above dispensed with the need.

A few months after their marriage, Erica finally persuaded him that the constant rub of leather against his skin only made the irritation worse. He thought that the sole way to gain acceptance was to cover up his shame, when to her, the true visage of the man would always serve as a continual reminder of his honor. At first, many in town *had* given him curious stares, some even disgusted winces, but once his face became a regular sight, the townspeople behaved as if the scars didn't exist, as she had hoped. Strangers didn't show the same regard to the town's deputy, but Christopher no longer minded the stares. If asked how he got the scars while in Erica's presence, she always made sure to relate how her husband acted with bravery, running into a burning building to save lives. That always earned him altered looks of admiration and respect, and from Christopher toward her, a look of sheer adoration.

"Look at me, Mama! Do I look like a bandit now, too, like Papa did when you chased him through the forest?"

Erica quirked a sober brow at her husband, who shrugged, his seeming innocence a farce. His eyes fairly glowed with warmth and danced with mischief. Whenever he looked at her like that, Erica forgot to think, sometimes to breathe, her insides melting like warm butter. But with the children present, she managed to preserve a grain of sense.

"I do hope you kept the content of our adventurous tale fit for young ears?"

Christopher tipped her chin, dropping a light kiss to her chagrined lips. "Of course," he whispered. "We wouldn't want them to know what a little spitfire their mother truly is, would we?"

Desperately trying to curb a smile, she swatted his arm, and he chuckled low in his throat.

"Will Grandpa and Grandma Chandler and Grandpa Waverly come visit later?" Sarah piped up. "Since it's my eighth birthday and all, I want to sing for them the song you both taught me."

"With the celebration into the twentieth century, Grandpa Waverly is very busy at the paper, but said he would try." Erica felt confident he would show, knowing how earnestly he endeavored to make time for his family. Both her fathers did. "Grandpa and Grandma Chandler should be here soon."

Erica gathered the remains of their picnic lunch. Christopher helped, and Sarah carefully folded the cloth in precise corners.

"Go on ahead," he told the children, "and take the basket with you. I want to speak with your mother."

"Don't wake your baby sister!" Erica called out, knowing her words were in vain as she watched their two lively young ones run, giggling, while holding the basket between them.

She laughed helplessly. Christopher took her hands, drawing her to turn his way.

"You're as beautiful as the day I met you."

"Oh, I'm sure I was a sight. Soil on my face, in my hair, and on my dress."

"In the eye of the beholder, remember?"

The sudden change of his mood, the sincerity in his eyes, and the warmth of his tone and embrace caused her heart to flutter. Married nine years to this man, and he could still make her senses stir at the sound of his voice or a simple touch. Even just upon entering a room.

"Any regrets?" His hands at her waist pulled her closer.

"Never." Willingly she went into his arms, her palms cradling his face. "There's no room in my heart for anything but the happiness I've found here with you, Christopher."

"In that, my angel, we are in one accord."

Their kiss came slow and gentle, passionate but restrained. Reluctantly they pulled away. Even when apart, the strength of their love knit them together, and she read that truth in his eyes as well. Erica once never would have believed it possible, but she loved Christopher more than on the day they wed.

Theirs had been an enchanting, breathless path of discovery in a life eagerly shared, of love and music, acceptance and forgiveness, lessons that never ended, new ones always taking place of the old. Life with Christopher hadn't always been easy, but it was forever inspired. Their fiery natures sometimes sparked heated arguments; at other times, passionate embraces or tender ones that burned like a gentle flame. With the arrival of little Sarah, their shared path had taken different and heartwarming, sometimes highly exasperating turns that only grew more complicated with each child they conceived, and likely always would, should God bless them with more.

And she wouldn't trade one second of this life for any other.

The jangle of a distant harness led them both to look up the path at an approaching wagon.

They smiled to see the figures of her father and Nora sitting side by side, another unexpected tale of love unmasked. Erica and Christopher shared a look of tender promise and clasped hands, moving forward to greet their guests.

In truth, she realized they had barely tapped the surface of their own story, and Erica looked forward to each of the many more exciting chapters to come.

* * * * *

REQUEST YOUR FREE BOOKS!

2 FREE CHRISTIAN NOVELS
PLUS 2
FREE
MYSTERY GIFTS

♡

HEARTSONG
PRESENTS

YES! Please send me 2 Free Heartsong Presents novels and my 2 FREE mystery gifts (gifts are worth about $10). After receiving them, if I don't wish to receive any more books I can return the shipping statement marked "cancel." If I don't cancel, I will receive 4 brand-new novels every month and be billed just $4.24 per book. That's a savings of 20% off the cover price. It's quite a bargain! Shipping and handling is just 50¢ per book in the U.S.* I understand that accepting the 2 free books and gifts places me under no obligation to buy anything. I can always return a shipment and cancel at any time. Even if I never buy another book, the two free books and gifts are mine to keep forever.

159 HDN FT97

Name _____ (PLEASE PRINT) _____

Address _____ Apt. # _____

City _____ State _____ Zip _____

Signature (if under 18, a parent or guardian must sign) _____

Mail to the **Reader Service:**
IN U.S.A.: P.O. Box 1867, Buffalo, NY 14240-1867

Not valid for current subscribers to Heartsong Presents books.

* Terms and prices subject to change without notice. Prices do not include applicable taxes. Sales tax applicable in N.Y. This offer is limited to one order per household. All orders subject to credit approval. Credit or debit balances in a customer's account(s) may be offset by any other outstanding balance owed by or to the customer. Please allow 4 to 6 weeks for delivery. Offer available while quantities last. Offer valid only in the U.S.

Your Privacy—The Reader Service is committed to protecting your privacy. Our Privacy Policy is available online at www.ReaderService.com or upon request from the Reader Service.

We make a portion of our mailing list available to reputable third parties that offer products we believe may interest you. If you prefer that we not exchange your name with third parties, or if you wish to clarify or modify your communication preferences, please visit us at www.ReaderService.com/consumerschoice or write to us at Reader Service Preference Service, P.O. Box 9062, Buffalo, NY 14269. Include your complete name and address.

HSP12

REQUEST YOUR FREE BOOKS!

2 FREE INSPIRATIONAL NOVELS
PLUS 2
FREE
MYSTERY GIFTS

Love Inspired

YES! Please send me 2 FREE Love Inspired® novels and my 2 FREE mystery gifts (gifts are worth about $10). After receiving them, if I don't wish to receive any more books, I can return the shipping statement marked "cancel." If I don't cancel, I will receive 6 brand-new novels every month and be billed just $4.49 per book in the U.S. or $4.99 per book in Canada. That's a savings of at least 22% off the cover price. It's quite a bargain! Shipping and handling is just 50¢ per book in the U.S. and 75¢ per book in Canada.* I understand that accepting the 2 free books and gifts places me under no obligation to buy anything. I can always return a shipment and cancel at any time. Even if I never buy another book, the two free books and gifts are mine to keep forever. 105/305 IDN FVW5

Name _____ (PLEASE PRINT) _____

Address _____ Apt. # _____

City _____ State/Prov. _____ Zip/Postal Code _____

Signature (if under 18, a parent or guardian must sign) _____

Mail to the **Reader Service:**
IN U.S.A.: P.O. Box 1867, Buffalo, NY 14240-1867
IN CANADA: P.O. Box 609, Fort Erie, Ontario L2A 5X3

**Are you a subscriber to Love Inspired books
and want to receive the larger-print edition?
Call 1-800-873-8635 or visit www.ReaderService.com.**

* Terms and prices subject to change without notice. Prices do not include applicable taxes. Sales tax applicable in N.Y. Canadian residents will be charged applicable taxes. Offer not valid in Quebec. This offer is limited to one order per household. Not valid for current subscribers to Love Inspired books. All orders subject to credit approval. Credit or debit balances in a customer's account(s) may be offset by any other outstanding balance owed by or to the customer. Please allow 4 to 6 weeks for delivery. Offer available while quantities last.

Your Privacy—The Reader Service is committed to protecting your privacy. Our Privacy Policy is available online at www.ReaderService.com or upon request from the Reader Service.

We make a portion of our mailing list available to reputable third parties that offer products we believe may interest you. If you prefer that we not exchange your name with third parties, or if you wish to clarify or modify your communication preferences, please visit us at www.ReaderService.com/consumerchoice or write to us at Reader Service Preference Service, P.O. Box 9062, Buffalo, NY 14269. Include your complete name and address.

LIDIR12